THE 9 DARK HOURS

THE 9 DARK HOURS

Lenore Glen Offord

Felony & Mayhem Press • New York

All the characters and events portrayed in this work are fictitious.

THE 9 DARK HOURS

A Felony & Mayhem mystery

PRINTING HISTORY
First edition (Duell, Sloan and Pearce): 1941
First paperback edition (Bruin): 2012
Felony & Mayhem edition: 2018

ISBN: 978-1-63194-119-1

Manufactured in the United States of America

Library of Congress Cataloging-in-Publication Data

Names: Offord, Lenore Glen, 1905-1991, author.
Title: The 9 dark hours / Lenore Glen Offord.
Other titles: Nine dark hours
Description: Felony & Mayhem edition. | New York : Felony & Mayhem Press,
2017.
Identifiers: LCCN 2017039691 | ISBN 9781631941191 (softcover)
Subjects: LCSH: Psychological fiction. | GSAFD: Suspense fiction. | Mystery
fiction.
Classification: LCC PS3529.F42 A15 2017 | DDC 813/.52--dc23
LC record available at https://lccn.loc.gov/2017039691

With love to
TANTE
Who once made an innocent journey
to the city of San Francisco

The icon above says you're holding a copy of a book in the Felony & Mayhem "Vintage" category. These books were originally published prior to about 1965, and feature the kind of twisty, ingenious puzzles beloved by fans of Agatha Christie and John Dickson Carr. If you enjoy this book, you may well like other "Vintage" titles from Felony & Mayhem Press.

Other "Vintage" titles from

FELONY & MAYHEM

ANTHONY BERKELEY
The Poisoned Chocolates Case

ELIZABETH DALY
Unexpected Night
Deadly Nightshade
Murders in Volume 2
The House without the Door
Evidence of Things Seen
Nothing Can Rescue Me
Arrow Pointing Nowhere
The Book of the Dead
Any Shape or Form
Somewhere in the House
The Wrong Way Down
Night Walk
The Book of the Lion
And Dangerous to Know
Death and Letters
The Book of the Crime

NGAIO MARSH
A Man Lay Dead
Enter a Murderer
The Nursing Home Murders
Death in Ecstasy
Vintage Murder
Artists in Crime
Death in a White Tie
Overture to Death
Death at the Bar
Surfeit of Lampreys
Death and the Dancing Footman
Colour Scheme
Died in the Wool
Final Curtain
Swing, Brother, Swing
Night at the Vulcan
Spinsters in Jeopardy
Scales of Justice
Death of a Fool
Singing in the Shrouds
False Scent
Hand in Glove
Dead Water
Killer Dolphin
Clutch of Constables
When in Rome
Tied Up in Tinsel
Black as He's Painted
Last Ditch
A Grave Mistake
Photo Finish
Light Thickens
Collected Short Mysteries

PATRICIA MOYES
Dead Men Don't Ski
The Sunken Sailor
Death on the Agenda
Murder à la Mode

LENORE GLEN OFFORD
Skeleton Key
The Glass Mask
The Smiling Tiger
My True Love Lies

THE 9 DARK HOURS

ONE

Perfect Gentle Knight

MY NAME IS Cameron Ferris. On a driver's license I'm described economically: "Sex, F. Race, White. Married? No." Up to the night of February 14, that was practically my life story. I have a few details to add to it now.

Just after Christmas, coming over on the ferry from an early morning train, I'd had my first glimpse of San Francisco. That day was clear, and the white towers climbing up and down the city's hills were washed in clean gold. The red bridge and the silver bridge flashed in the light, soaring over Golden Gate and Bay. "Ah, California and sunshine," I'd said to myself—though fortunately not aloud. "Ah, San Francisco, city of adventure!"

That, until February 11, had been my last look at clear sunlight. Any adventure I had found you could have put in your eye.

I'll admit I was looking for it in an unlikely place. Maybe if I'd been an artist, starving in a shack on North Beach, there would have been more scope for the imagination; but I'm an ordinary person, with no artistic talents and a hearty appetite, and a job—any job—was good enough for the present. Caya & Co., Wholesale Hardware, needed a filing clerk, and Miss Ferris was in, as from Jan. 1.

Sometimes the advertisements try to make us believe that there's high romance in all types of business, could one but see below the surface. "Think," they might say of a concern such as ours, "think of this carload of widgets, resting in Caya's warehouse. Picture the far-flung territory over which they will eventually be scattered. The farmer on the lonely Dakota plains waits eagerly for the new widget without which his tractor will not run. The shipyards, springing up like magic from Maine to California, could not be built without widgets. From Alaska to South America—"

You know the sort of thing. Maybe I could have worked up an interest in Caya's merchandise, but I never so much as laid an eye on it. As I went to work I saw the wholesale district, dun-gray, huge, hideous and dripping with rain. Inside the office my nose was glued to a filing cabinet.

I did manage for a while to extract a mild amusement from the orders I handled. Caya's sold nails and tools and model trains, of course, as any hardware firm does; but in addition to these there would be orders, in habit-forming quantities, for the most incredible things like barswingles and Hagedorn clamps. Don't be literal, of course those weren't their names; they just sounded like that, and I'll never know what they actually are. Somebody named Flaherty would demand 100 gross Hagedorn clamps, for delivery not later than Jan. 31. Well, I'd think, there was plenty of time to pack up that order even if the warehouse boys had to pick it out clamp by clamp. But what would Flaherty do with it?

That amusement, I knew, would pall before long; but there was one bright spot on my horizon, not scintillating, you understand, but a perceptible glow. This was Mr. Tripp, the head of the order department in which I worked.

Anyone would have to admit that he was a good-looking lad, with brown hair and hazel eyes and a profile that may not have been Barrymore's but showed a distinct Grecian cast. He was kind, he was courteous and patient in teaching me my job—though it wasn't hard to learn after one had grasped Mr. Caya's peculiar system of doing business—and I thought he approved of me. Very well, then, I knew it.

At first I had wondered what this handsome youngish creature was doing here. After a time I found out. Near-sighted eyes had kept him out of the draft; and as for his surroundings, they were meat and drink to him. Roger Tripp actually loved the wholesale hardware business. He put his whole soul into it, and would certainly go far. Within ten years, doubtless, he would be manufacturing his own barswingles in an improved form.

Before I had spent three weeks among the files, it was plain that if I wanted to hand out the least little bit of encouragement I could work up beside him and eventually become the hardware queen.

It was proved to me, along toward the last of January, by a slight dust-up I had with old Mr. Caya. It was our first personal contact, though from the study of his astonishing filing system I felt somewhat acquainted with the character of my employer. I owed my job to his idiosyncrasies, and to the complicated method he'd invented in the days of his fiery youth, somewhere back in the nineties.

Every firm that sent us an order was expected to indicate a deadline for delivery. The order forms, after being copied, cross-indexed, handled and re-handled, were placed in the warehouse file—arranged not alphabetically, nor in order of receipt, but according to the deadline dates. Thus the warehouse boys knew exactly how fast they'd have to work, and could catch their breaths and enjoy a few crap games between bouts of shipping.

I don't know if anyone else does business this way. In our case it seemed practical enough, since Caya's proudly boasted that barring acts of God no customer had ever been forced to wait for the filling of his order. The perfect record had to be broken some time, I suppose; and for a while it looked as if that distinction had been reserved for me.

One rainy Monday morning Mr. Caya sent for me, and I'd no sooner stepped inside his office than I felt about eight years old and convicted of throwing spitballs. In the embarrassed presence of a harried-looking stranger named Smith, of Mr. Caya's secretary, and of Roger Tripp with his hands full of duplicates and cross-file cards, Mr. Caya barked at me.

"'S Ferris. You've been handling the A to M orders."

I didn't deny that. Over the bristling white head, Mr. Tripp sent me an encouraging smile. He was a bit nervous himself. The boss hadn't enough energy to modernize his office, but plenty for taking the hide off employees.

"What did you learn first thing when you came here, huh? Orders filed by date for delivery. Don't interrupt me. You know that. That's the important thing to watch. It's all you have to watch."

Yes, I did. Yes, it was. Yes.

"Miss Ferris is new here," Mr. Tripp put in kindly.

"New! She's been here long enough to learn one simple little thing. I will not have carelessness. She can't learn to be accurate, she can leave. Mist' Smith, here, 's a busy man—came all the way over from Oakland to find out about that shipment to Flaherty. Telephoned twice, I told him shipment must be on its way, delay couldn't be our fault. Now I find out the warehouse men never *saw* that order. Hagedorn clamps, a hundred gross of 'em! Flaherty needs 'em bad, can't do a thing without—"

I said, "Mr. Caya, I remember that order. The goods were to be shipped on or before January thirty-first."

"Thirteenth, Miss Ferris, thirteenth! You looked at it and didn't see it! You copied it wrong, got it in the cross-files wrong! You've been told over and over—"

"I don't pretend to be infallible," I told him, "but I'm sure I made no mistake in this case."

"Godsakes, Miss Ferris, didn't you look at that date? January thirty-first is a Sunday!"

I stood my ground. "The order said not later than the thirty-first."

"Alibis, alibis!" Mr. Caya shouted. "Why don't you admit you're careless, instead of telling a pack of—"

The Celtic blood of the Ferrises went up to 211° F. "I do not lie my way out of mistakes," I said, with intent to blister. Mr. Caya began slowly and visibly to swell, and creaked round in his swivel chair.

And then Roger Tripp, bless his heart, came to the rescue. "I know that's so," he said. "Miss Ferris has been here only a short time, but I've had a chance to observe her. She might be in error, but if so she'd admit it at once. I should call her—dependable."

The secretary rolled an eye at him and then at me. It seemed that the accolade had been bestowed.

Mr. Caya rounded on him. "And how, in that case, do you explain the date on those duplicates?"

Almost with bated breath, I offered a meek suggestion. Anywhere else they'd have tried it first, but not here. "Couldn't you find the original order?"

"Yes," Mr. Tripp said, "and that will prove it. I'll find it myself. It must be somewhere in the warehouse; I'll go down and put the fear of the Lord into those men!"

He was magnificent, striding out. The profile had never looked better to me.

Mr. Caya grudgingly told me I could sit down. For the next ten minutes, while the secretary industriously typed and the silent Mr. Smith looked out the window at a rain-lashed street, the old boy treated me to a speech on the importance of the Hagedorn clamps, without which Mr. Flaherty's building—whatever it might be—would inevitably fall down at once. He was as gruff as ever, but not so sure of his ground. There were no more aspersions.

The boys in the warehouse, I heard later, were having a refreshing cigarette and catching up on the adventures of Dick

Tracy when Roger, breathing flame, descended upon them. They were affronted, but reluctantly uncoiled their legs and joined in the search.

The Flaherty order was run to earth, way down in the pile of next week's jobs. The boys protested that they had lots of time on it, and what was all the shouting for? They were left expostulating to the vacant air. Mr. Tripp charged back to the office in triumph, bearing the original order. It was plainly dated January 31.

Mr. Caya, deflated, glared at him and me as if he suspected us of conniving at a forgery. The harried Mr. Smith looked at the date, and his frown deepened. "But—our carbon!" he cried wildly. "Our carbon of this order read thirteenth! That's what put us off, because we—but how on earth could the original form be different?"

Then he turned and stared at Mr. Caya, and his voice changed. "Has this happened with other people's orders—anyone's but ours?"

"Never happened before, not in the forty years I've—"

"Well, it's not the first time we've been held up on this job. There have been other things. Last week there was a delay in shipping us some lumber—we thought it was just bad luck, but now I think I'd better look into it more closely. You know what it means, Mr. Caya, if we lose even a day."

"Bad business," said Mr. Caya perfunctorily. As long as the mistake wasn't ours, he didn't seem to care what happened.

I'd been waiting patiently for dismissal, and now it came, with a muttered apology from both men. Smith said, "I'm sure I didn't mean to—you know, these things have to be investigated."

Well, what would you have thought? Just what I did—that he was making heavy weather of a very small mystery. I never remembered to ask what Mr. Flaherty was constructing.

When I say that this incredibly dull episode marked the high point of my career in hardware, maybe you can guess what the rest of it was like.

There were, however, two aftereffects. Mr. Caya looked at me very hard whenever we met, and several times came and stood behind me as I worked, causing the Ferris teeth to grit. Also, from then on, in his own eyes as well as those of the whole department, Mr. Tripp became my protector and champion.

I didn't know whether or not to like this. These situations have a way of getting out of hand, and we were now at the stage where too much cordiality on my part might give him ideas. Handsome and steady and kind as he was, I wasn't sure that I was ready for any avowed interest. And yet, he had braved the old man and jeopardized his own position in my defense; there were times when I felt that he was really very sweet.

He took to coming round in slack moments, leaning on my desk and telling me the plot of the movie he'd seen the night before. Now and then disapproval was expressed. Sex dramas didn't please him, and as for Hedy Lamarr and Ann Sheridan, they might be full of oomph but that wasn't his type at all. There was something unwholesome about them.

This confidence, accompanied by a look indicating that the type he preferred was sitting not three feet away, gave me a quite ridiculous feeling of annoyance. He should have made me feel that Lamarr might be glamorous, but that in his eyes I could make her look like Carrie Nation. Nobody wants to be told she can't compete in a major league.

That was unreasonable, of course. I knew it.

You've seen girls like me, who because of some directness of look or sturdiness of carriage seem boyish, no matter how many curves they may have. It's something to do with straight blondish hair in a neat bun at the nape of the neck, or with heavy eyebrows a lot darker than the hair,—or, more likely, with firm pink cheeks that owe nothing to the cosmetic counter. You may have enjoyed looking at those girls—I don't believe my face has ever frightened any babies—but what were the words that came into your mind as a description? I know. Solid, wholesome, dependable. That's an accurate thumbnail sketch of Cameron Ferris' outward appearance, and if you think I am complimenting myself, ask any woman if those are not the three most loathsome adjectives in the language.

A person who looks like that is more than likely to lead a solid, wholesome life, no matter how great her craving for a bit of caviar in the shape of adventure. As for playing the lead in a sex drama, my kind of face is like a mask. There had been some men, certainly, who had professed to be in love with me; but I knew they saw nothing but the mask, and the qualities it promised were all they wanted. The ones I could have loved never troubled to find out what was behind the face. They saw Merideth instead, my lovely sister whose looks do not belie her capacity for passion.

Jock Crosley, whom she married, once said, "Ronnie looks like a pale pink zinnia."—You know, the sturdy cheerful flowers in your grandmother's garden. Poor lamb, he thought he was pleasing me! By that time I was almost over my unspoken, unguessed-at love for Jock, but I think that speech completed the cure.

And yet that experience had given me a queer complex about love. I knew what it should be, and felt unwilling to accept substitutes. I wanted something I wasn't likely to get, the kind of romance that stings and sparkles, that—oh, well, why describe it? It's what everyone wants, and a few achieve.

If I didn't get over the complex, it was going to spoil Roger for me. In a way, that was too bad. I could be what he wanted: a cheerful companion, a good housekeeper, a mother for his handsome children. I could grow fond of him. There were times when I thought that was all I was meant to have out of marriage—and times when I rebelled at the thought. But sometime soon, I should have to make up my mind.

So January went out and February washed in on a torrent of rain, and I went on filing orders and did not ask Mr. Tripp to call on me at my new apartment. Maybe he would have hesitated to come, anyway. He was touchingly thoughtful of my reputation.

When he spoke to me about the change of address, nothing could have been kinder; not fussy at all, just interested. It was my fault that it happened to irritate me.

"Miss Ferris," he said one afternoon late in January, "I see by your registration card that you're no longer staying at the girls' club. There wasn't any trouble, I hope?"

"None at all," said I. The girls had nearly talked me to death, but you couldn't call that trouble—not compared with a bombing raid.

"You're sharing this apartment with a friend?"

"No. I'm alone."

"I see." Roger was silent for a moment. Then he said, "Of course you want to be independent; but—could we pretend for a minute that I'm your father?"

"I'm afraid not—unless you were a very precocious youth."

He laughed. "Make it elder brother, then."

Not so elder, either. I am twenty-eight, though I love to tell myself I don't look it.

"You see," he went on, "Mrs. Brent is married, and Miss Hamilton lives with her family. As members of my department, I'd feel responsible for them, too, if they were alone."

Oh yeah?

"But you're—well, I know you're too sensible for any of the obvious dangers, letting strange men pick you up, anything like that; but do you think it's quite wise to—uh—to set yourself entirely adrift, with no protection from older people?"

Sensible. There's another fightin' word. "Why, Mr. Tripp," I said, "nothing can happen to me. Were you thinking of the apartment? It's quiet and respectable, and close to town."

"Oh, I feel sure you'd never choose a place that wasn't respectable. It's your being alone that worries me. You're a stranger in town, and I—well, I don't like to think of your going home at night to a lonely room, with no one to—well, to care about your welfare, or to help if anything should go wrong."

I said I hadn't been ill in years.

"I was thinking of something besides illness," he said soberly. "This is a big, cosmopolitan city, and—dreadful things can happen to young women, you know. I beg your pardon? Did you say something?"

I had muttered "No such luck," under my breath, but now I gave him a smile and returned, "Really, I enjoy being alone."

He wasn't convinced, but the elder-brother gag couldn't be carried to the point of giving orders. Preparing to leave, he murmured, "I can't feel that it is quite—well, quite—"

"Oh, I'm perfectly safe," said I brightly, "but thank you so much for your interest!"

No such luck was right, I reflected glumly as I went back to work. By nature I simply was not the kind of person to whom interesting things happen.

I'd mentioned to Mr. Tripp that I'd be much happier if my employer would give up his habit of suddenly appearing round corners and glaring at me balefully. Roger at once jumped to the conclusion that my nerves were shattered. He sympathized with me kindly, and explained that Mr. Caya didn't mean anything by it, that was only his way of making tacit apology, perhaps studying me in view of promotion.

I found both these theories highly unlikely, but Roger said that could be laid to my Nerves. He'd see what could be done.

A day or so later he came round to whisper that he'd wangled me an extra holiday. The office would normally close on Friday, Lincoln's Birthday, but the next day also could be mine for free. Why didn't I go away somewhere—get away from it all?

This was extremely good of him, and fitted in well enough with my own ideas. I'd felt for some time that a tree would be a refreshing sight, and the week beginning February 7 had offered a breathing space between storms. The weather man was not sticking his neck out, but he hinted that we *might* have some sunshine, unless of course it should start raining again.

"Thank you, Mr. Tripp," I said. We were still Mr. and Miss to each other, but I felt that any minute he might begin to call me Ronnie; outside the office only, that should go without saying. "I may do just that."

"Good," said Roger, obviously pleased. "Now, then. Have you any place in mind?"

I hadn't quite foreseen this, and lacked the presence of mind to lie.

"Then I know a resort that would be the very place for you. It's not expensive, it's very quiet and decent, and we know the landlady. Mother has stayed there several times, and she recommends it heartily. It's—really, it's a home away from home."

I made an indeterminate sound.

"Real country, too," he pressed me, "though it's not so very far away. The transportation is splendid. I can tell you just what buses to take; I believe the schedule is right here in my wallet."

He was so eager, and meant so well, and his nice hazel eyes beamed on me so kindly, that I hadn't the heart to reject these suggestions. Was that significant, that I should hesitate to hurt him?

On the other hand, maybe you'd like to make something out of my next impulse. This was to say, "Mr. Tripp, I intend to pass this weekend in a gambling hell, the croupier has been my friend for years. You may take your country hotel and your landlady and your bus schedule, and you may—"

But that was exceedingly coarse, and I was surprised at myself. He's really sweet, I thought.

TWO

It Rains into the Sea

THE BOARDING HOUSE was all that Roger had said of it: respectable, safe and quiet. And oh, was it dull!

And oh, what weather! I could have done better standing under a waterfall. No doubt I'd brought that on myself, since at the last minute I had included a raincoat and rubbers in my luggage. But did I poke a hole in the roof right over my bed, so that on Sunday afternoon it sprung a disastrous leak? No.

Of course, nobody depends on dry weather in the middle of a California winter. I should have known better; but when you've nearly impoverished yourself for a country weekend, and it becomes a washout in every sense of the word, you have a right to grumble and to think that Salem, Oregon, was never like this.

The motherly woman who ran the dump said reasonably enough that she couldn't get the roof fixed until the rain let up, and it was too bad that she had no other room to give me, but we could move the bed and put a tin pan under the leak, to catch the water as it came down drip drip drip.

I said no, thanks, that I'd go home on Sunday evening instead of the next morning.

Funny, funny, to think it was as simple as that.

As inducement to mental comfort, I do not recommend a mixture of guilt and morose annoyance. Those made up my frame of mind as, in a pouring rain, I waited for the bus. It's worse than this in London, I thought; and the voice inside me, which is always arguing, shot back—How do you know?

The bus came, its wheels shooting up fans of water from a young lake in the highway, and I climbed aboard. When I'd paid my fare just sixty-seven cents was left in my purse, but pay checks were due the next day so I wasn't worried. The rain coursed in streams off my hooded cellophane raincoat as I stumbled to a seat; all the other passengers must have been as wet as I, because the bus seemed to be filled with steam and scented with damp wool and rubber. It was dark. You couldn't see through the misted windows, and nobody was talking.

Little by little, as we rode silent and swaying, my annoyance fell away and another mood took its place. Maybe you know how oddly disembodied one can seem on a long quiet drive through darkness. There isn't any sense of time, and space is something that flows effortlessly under the wheels. Add to that the peculiar Sunday-night pause, when the week is being wound up so it can start ticking again the next morning, and with no effort at all you can feel like the little man who wasn't there.

I thought dreamily about Caya's, and the order system, and Roger Tripp, and began to wonder if any of them existed except in my imagination. If the thought of Roger had caused the least stir of my pulse, I'd have been sure he was real.

Come right down to it, was *I* real? Was this Cameron Ferris, here on this spot, or had I left my actual self with my family in Oregon? Here I had no background, no roots, no ties. *This sycamore tree simply ceases to be, when there's no one about in the Quad.*

It was partly homesickness, I think; nostalgia for something I couldn't go back to because it didn't exist anymore. Everything ends sometime, including other people's need of you. Of course they had done their best to pretend, Father and my nice new middle-aged stepmother in Salem, and the Crosleys in Portland—my lovely sister Merideth and her husband Jock and their three babies that I'd practically brought up to their present age. Both families had asked me to make my home with them. Naturally I couldn't do it, no matter how deep and sincere our affection for each other. I'd wanted to get clean away.

But there's lots of loneliness in complete freedom!

If I believed Roger really needed me, that would be something. I might—I might consider giving him some encouragement.

I never felt oppressed by my family's dependence. We three Ferrises were very close together, from the time when Mother died of the flu and Father came home from the war. I was only six and Merideth nine, but Father, undismayed, took on our upbringing. Very early we learned to do our own thinking and make our own way. Anyone of Scottish, Irish and English heritage is not quick to let himself be pushed around, but I may say that we were tougher than most.

Father stood by us, and taught us to divide fairly and not to show it when we got hurt. We adored him and each other. It wasn't duty that brought Merideth home from college when Dad's real-estate business fell to pieces in the Depression; it was because we'd always shared everything that she insisted I should have my chance at the University, working my way through of necessity but free to do it because she was at home. No more was it duty that made me give up my teaching job, seven years later, and come home to nurse Father when his arthritis crippled him. It was, too, the most natural thing on earth that when Jock Crosley's architecture firm folded he and Merideth and the two babies—with another one in the offing—should move for a time into the big Ferris house, that we'd kept because we couldn't sell it. I had little chance for a life of my own, but because we all belonged together I didn't mind.

Belonging to somebody once more might be all I needed. I'd be happy enough with the safety and security, the home and babies.

—Not anyone's home! Not just anyone's babies! the argumentative voice reminded me.

I told the voice severely that Roger would do very well indeed. Roger would be the answer to many a maiden's prayer. Why not mine?

Maybe if my life hadn't always been made up of safe routine, I'd appreciate him more. Maybe the gift of one thrilling moment, one bit of excitement that I hadn't made laboriously for myself would show me life in its true proportion.

Five minutes later, to my utter astonishment, I thought the moment had arrived. I'd settled back with my eyes closed, trying to imagine Mr. Tripp in the bosom of our ribald family, when the bus pulled up onto a shoulder of the road and the lights abruptly went out.

I sat up hopefully. What was it? A flood? A holdup? My sixty-seven cents, I felt, would have been well lost in this latter cause.

That fancy was shattered before I'd fairly got going on it. The driver announced in a casual voice that the generator musta burned out; and indeed, it was even so.

Take that, Miss Ferris.

There was a brief flurry of alarm among the suddenly aroused passengers, which the driver, used to such emergencies, soon quieted. He plodded up the road to the nearest telephone, and inside of twenty minutes a relief bus came along and picked us up. The efficiency of this machine age may yet be the death of romance.

We were all awakened, though, by the change, and in the general reshuffle of travelers and luggage the trip took on a more social air. A billowy old lady stuffed herself into the seat beside me, and during the rest of the trip she babbled cheerfully at me without once stopping. I heard all about her home, and her family, and the visit she had just been paying to her daughter and her son-in-law, Joe. I could just see Joe. He'd be the counterpart of all the other men, besides Roger, whom I'd met in the past six weeks; middle-aged, heavy, good-natured, with lodge emblems in their buttonholes and snapshots of the Missus and the kiddies in their wallets.

My inner voice inquired if Roger might not be just like that in ten years' time.

This Joe, it seemed, was something of a wag. Whenever she bought something new, said the old lady with a deprecating giggle not devoid of pride, he always teased her. This time it was just a little suitcase she'd picked up at a sale, but Joe got off on one of his killingly funny tangents and accused her of all sorts of crazy things. First he'd decided she must be the Barefoot Burglar who'd been harrying the East Bay residents. Then, when that joke wore thin, he said that maybe she'd accepted bribes from enemy agents and was preparing to become a spy. This was based on something he'd been reading in the newspaper. Had I ever heard of anyone as silly as Joe?

I made a gentle sound to indicate I hadn't.

"They're always talking about the Fifth Column, getting people all het up," said my companion blithely. "I don't believe a word of it—but it's interesting reading. I told Joe, just for that if anyone tried to bribe me I'd give 'em the plans of his overall factory."

Frisky old soul, I thought with a grin. She'd probably love it if she had the chance—Mata Hari at seventy-five. I had to admit, though, that Joe's factory wasn't in immediate danger.

She went on talking, talking. I lost the thread presently. The bus was hot, and there's something hypnotic about an effortless flow of words; after a while you get deaf to their meaning. Her soft elderly flesh encroached more and more on my share of the seat.

And now the dream-like contemplation had left me, and I was suddenly awake and in discomfort. Crossly and unfairly, I thought—this is all Roger Tripp's fault.

Real or not, I couldn't keep the man out of my head, probably because he was the only one around. Very well, if he would haunt me, I'd blame him for this miserable trip.

It was especially unfair because he'd given me explicit directions about coming home. It wasn't safe for me to go wandering through dark streets alone, late at night. There was a bus in the morning which would get me to Caya's in time for work.

I'd said, "That's cutting it rather fine, Mr. Tripp. I'd prefer to sleep in my own bed on Sunday night."

"Please," he'd said very charmingly, "do as I ask, so I shan't have to—well, to worry about you, and wonder if you're safe."

Somewhat touched by this interest, I'd gone all weak and given him the promise. That was where my recent feeling of guilt had arisen.

"—As you know if you've been in San Francisco, dear," the old lady beside me was saying. I hadn't the slightest idea what I was supposed to know. "Or—you don't live there, do you?"

"Yes," I said—my sole contribution to the evening's talk.

She shook her head. "You don't look it. I'd have said you were a farm girl, with those lovely pink cheeks of yours and all—so wholesome-looking."

I turned inwardly livid; but you cannot paste old ladies in the snoot. It was with great relief that I saw we were now approaching the terminal.

"Well! We're in, and what a short trip it's seemed," said she; and from under the seat pulled out the black leather dressing-case which, when the luggage was transferred, I had spotted as mine.

"See, this is what I told you about," she cried. "This is what I bought at the sale, and they put my initials on it free."

I gazed at it, blinked and gazed again. No matter how you look at it, my initials are not M. M.

There was no doubt that the case was hers, and I watched her trot off without even mentioning that there was any difficulty. All that the subsequent research and questioning and fuss established was that my small suitcase had somehow been overlooked in the transfer.

It gave me a sort of gloomy satisfaction. Aha, I thought, didn't I tell you? That's the only sort of thing that happens to me, ever. Fifteen pieces of baggage in that compartment, and mine was the one that got pushed into a corner. That puts the lid on this weekend.

—The Valentine's Day Massacre, I added for good measure, and then realized with a start that these words had come out aloud, for the clerk who was taking down particulars jumped and stared at me reproachfully. This habit of talking to myself was one that I'd acquired only lately, and I had no doubt that someday it would land me behind bars.

Disentangled at last from the red tape of the claims office, I left the terminal, feeling oddly light and unburdened with only my handbag to carry. My face was lashed with rain as I walked the few blocks to Market, which seemed cold and deserted on this wild night, and caught an O'Farrell, Jones and Hyde cable car. It was ready to start; they held it for me while I ran the last twenty yards and scrambled onto the step. The cable, sounding impatient, clicked and grumbled in the slot beneath, and we went trundling off along the wet streets, their pavements shining with rain-blurred reflections of light. It was early yet, only about ten, and some of the liquor and drug stores were still open. The gay red and white of valentine displays had disappeared, and the druggists' windows showed utilitarian designs of hot water bottles and cold cures. In a very few minutes we had come to the apartment district.

There were miles and miles of apartment houses, marching up and down these hills. They were much alike, four- and five-story buildings with regular corrugations of bay windows striping their facades. I looked at them through the rain-spattered windows. As usual, the houses looked back at me without rancor or welcome, without recognition.

I don't like to admit that anything can get me down, but the city of San Francisco had come very near to doing just that.

Its size and aspect were not too formidable, but what terrified me was its huge impersonality. The moment I left the office I became nobody. I had fallen here as a spatter of rain drops into the ocean, changing neither the tide nor the taste of the brine. I had, I thought, been absorbed without a ripple.

That phrase had a familiar ring. Wasn't it what they said of persons who disappeared?

I got off the cable car and climbed the block and a half to my apartment house. The street was quiet even at this comparatively early hour. Very few automobiles were out tonight. In a darkened doorway across the street, a cigarette end glowed and faded and was flung down.

Here was my own door, and here was another small annoyance. The slip of card bearing my name had disappeared from its slot in the row of foyer mailboxes. If it had fallen out it could be replaced in a minute, but the box was empty and I decided not to bother tonight.

I let myself into the dimly lighted foyer of "El Central." It was an apartment house like dozens of others. When I found my job at Caya's and left the girls' club, I had gone flat-hunting. In this region, on the edge of the business district, the available places were dismally similar, and after I'd inspected eight or ten identical velour chesterfields and fringed floor lamps, it had appeared to me that price was the only basis of choice. Mrs. Ulrichson, the landlady of El Central, had looked me over carefully, and for some unknown reason had come down on her first quotation of rent. I had searched no farther, only indicating a preference for the chesterfield and bargain-basement rug in 4-D over their twins in 2-D, two floors below and twice as dark. (The new gen'man in 4-C had felt the same way, said Mrs. Ulrichson; top floor or nothin' for him.) The choice meant a climb every night, since there was no elevator in this house; the building next door had one, but charged five dollars more a month, which decided me at once.

The well-known Woman's Touch had only slightly ameliorated the horror of the taupe velour, but my one room on the fourth floor back was not unpleasant after I'd unpacked my own lamps and pictures and hidden those of Mrs. Ulrichson's choice in the depths of the dressing room. I knew exactly what I'd find when I opened the door of 4-D, and went to the left down the little inner hall, and switched on the light in the one large room which, with kitchenette and bath, made up my quarters. The picture of Merideth and her three boys would be waiting for me, and the bronze luster pitcher in which I tried to keep flowers, the four cactus plants in four little pots of sand on the windowsill, and my books and sewing basket.

Radios boomed from behind closed doors as I climbed the stairs, and I could figure the time with fair accuracy. The Richfield Reporter was just sandwiching a commercial between the halves of his fifteen-minute program, which began at ten. On my own floor, the top one, music flooded from 4-A at the head of the stairs. Two flights down I had heard it begin, *"O Freunde, nicht diese Töne,"* and could only suppose that Mrs. Pitman was too busy to turn it off. She was the only one of my neighbors to whom I'd ever spoken, and on the strength of our brief visit I fancied she would not care for that portion of the Ninth Symphony which is based upon the *Ode to Joy*. Sure enough, as I came level with the door, a glorious shout of *"Freude!"* was abruptly cut off. I could almost hear Mrs. Pitman moaning "Classical!" as she wrenched at the knob.

I turned to the right, down the corridor with the dingy carpet which I had traversed more than fifty times in the past month, so that I knew its red and green pattern by heart. The other apartments on this floor were quiet: 4-B, on my left, 4-C on the right farther down, which housed a man named Spelvin, and my own 4-D at the far end. Around the corner from the stairwell was one more door, behind which the stairs continued to the roof.

The details of this hall were so familiar that they registered only on my subconscious eye: brass letters and numerals screwed into wood, and the board creaking under the carpet as I passed 4-B. I reached my end of the hall, fitted my key into the Yale lock and turned it. The lock worked with surprising ease and quiet, and I thought that Mrs. Ulrichson, in a fit of unusual energy, must have been busy with the oil can.

The door closed behind me, I clicked on the hall light and bent to take off my galoshes. "Home again," said I aloud to the apartment which had heard so many of my soliloquies.

It was then that I noticed the illumination in the living room. I couldn't remember leaving that light on—funny!

I walked down the short hall and flung open the door. My hand left the knob, and was arrested in mid-motion; poised in the act of taking a step, I halted, shaken by a horrible qualm.

This was not my apartment.

The furniture was in the wrong places, there were pictures on the walls, and a terrible floor lamp swung its bead fringe over the velour armchair. On the sofa there sat, also transfixed in astonishment, a perfectly strange man.

THREE

One Cat Too Many

I THINK I HAVE never been so frightened.

There are dreams like that, in which a familiar place goes distorted and queer, with doors where there should be no doors. The dream forces you to go searching among them, despairingly, and you know that one of them will open on a bottomless black space roaring with unfriendly winds. I'd had those nightmares sometimes, and wakened from them with a moment of sick terror.

But I wasn't asleep now, I couldn't be asleep! The rain was still wet on my coat, my cheeks stung with the transition from cold to warmth. I couldn't have imagined a radio commercial, nor the brass numbers on my door. The key that had opened it was real and tangible in my hand. If this was a dream, why didn't I wake?

The man was the first to recover from his surprise, and it gave him some advantage. All I had seen of him at first was a pair of soiled and disreputable flannel trousers, and startled blue eyes above the edge of an outspread newspaper. Now he put the paper aside and got to his feet. It seemed to take him a long time to rise to his full height, and his shoulders spread to an incredible width so that he loomed immense and alien in this strange room. I half expected him to go on growing, dissolving into a dark cloud that would come down on me in smothering weight.

You don't hear actual voices in your sleep, though. When he spoke, his voice was real—at once deep and soft and faintly husky. "Were you looking for someone?" he said courteously.

My own words caught in my throat. "I—no. I'm in my own—This is my apartment!" And then I added, foolishly, unsteadily, "Isn't it?"

"Afraid not," the man said. His eyes were cool; they were of the light blue that makes you think of sailors or aviators. Their expression was guarded as well as chilly. "As you see," he pointed out, "it's mine."

I gazed wildly around me. I knew now that I was awake, but a more unnerving doubt had taken possession of my mind, because all the evidence pointed to the truth of his words. There was a litter of books and papers on the table, and a framed photograph of a grim-faced woman propped up beside them. A pipe had been knocked out in an unfamiliar large ashtray, a leather jacket was flung across the arm of the chesterfield. Not a sign remained here to show that I had ever been in the apartment before; it was as if my name, written on a blackboard, had announced my claim—and had vanished at the touch of an eraser.

"I don't see how I can have made a mistake," my voice faltered. "This key opened the door."

I looked at the room again. Now that the first shock was over, the furniture even in its changed position once more appeared familiar; but it was the same taupe velour that prevailed throughout the house, that might have been found in a dozen other apartment buildings.

"Is—isn't this the top floor?" I asked.

The man said, "Yes," flatly. He was watching me with that same expression, his mouth set in a hard uncompromising line.

Now the doubt was growing. I rubbed my forehead hard, but that didn't help much. "It's not possible that I've gone crazy?" I thought, and to my great consternation realized that I had said it aloud. The man made no response, but his look took on an almost imperceptible shade of compassion.

"Do you mind if I look around?" I managed a somewhat braver tone, and turned to fling open the door beside me. The gesture, even to me, had the quality of desperation.

The dressing room was still there, the same shape and size, but that meant very little. There were a few masculine garments hanging on the rods, and a pair of military brushes on the built-in chest of drawers at the end. A battered Gladstone bag stood on the low shelf where my big suitcase had been. Not a sign, not a sign! In the long mirror that backed the door I saw my own image, pallid and terrified.

"Look here," I said, turning back to the man, who stood motionless, "something's terribly wrong. I was in this apartment until Friday morning, and it was all right when I left it. They surely can't have rented it over my head and moved out all my belongings?"

"Not from this place," he said calmly. "I've been here for two weeks."

You never saw anyone look so large and steady and imperturbable. He was so solidly planted on his feet that I could well believe he'd been here for two weeks—or months, or years.

It was then that I remembered how the cable car had lurched as I boarded it. Could I, without realizing it, have struck my head? There were cases you read about, cases of amnesia and transfer of personality. Had I, Cameron Ferris—yes, I could remember my own name—really left that dull country boarding house, two hours ago, and come straight to this place—or had weeks passed since then, a space which had somehow been blotted from my memory? Might I have been wandering unknown and unsought for all that time, coming to just at this moment, blundering instinctively back to my apartment?

I couldn't help recalling that dreamy passage of time on the bus, the illusory sense that among those silent strangers I had lost my own identity. It might have felt just that way if I'd been gradually recovering from amnesia.

But I could *remember* that. The old lady and her conversation were vivid in my mind, and the clerk who'd asked for particulars about my suitcase. Equally clear was the memory of Thursday's work at the office. Why, there couldn't be anything wrong with me, I couldn't let myself think it!

Yet right then, for the first time, I was conscious of a curious duality of mind, doubt and certainty existing side by side, which was to stay with me in some measure through the whole night.

I'd have to pull myself together. "You moved in," I said slowly, "two weeks ago? How was the apartment furnished then?"

"Very much as it is now," he said.

"But—my suitcases, my clothes—they weren't here? What's become of my brown luster pitcher, and the balsam pillow on the chesterfield?"

"I don't know anything about them," the big man answered, and now there was a hint of impatience in his tone. I could see plainly enough what he expected; I was to admit that I'd made a mistake, and get out without further ado. If someone had burst in on me with as little ceremony, I could never have been so polite. Nonetheless, I had to persist.

"Did anyone tell you that the previous tenant had disappeared, mysteriously?" No, that was a mistake. Even as he moved his head in a negative gesture, I realized that I couldn't afford to make mistakes.

"This is the fourth floor," I made a fresh start. "My key opened the door."

He shrugged. "In these apartment houses, keys might be interchangeable."—Too patient, too polite, I thought suddenly.

"In Yale locks? I can't believe that. And if there'd been a key missing, wouldn't Mrs. Ulrichson have changed the lock?"

"Who is Mrs. Ulrichson?" His eyes seemed to measure me, as if probing for knowledge.

"Don't you know the landlady's name? —She's the one to settle this, of course. Will you get her, please, and ask her to come up?"

The man hesitated, and then gave a half laugh, the kind that means you've almost reached the end of your tether. He said, firmly but softly, "I don't know what to make of this. There is no landlady here. All my dealings have been with a man called Bassett, who runs this place. I am afraid, under the circumstances, that it won't do you the least good to see him."

"I must know, please!" I said, and looked at him as appealingly as I could. "You'll come downstairs with me, won't you? It won't take a minute to clear up this misunderstanding."

His face didn't change in the least, yet suddenly I knew that he was very reluctant to go. Now why? If he really thought me misguided or insane, the easiest way to get rid of me was to prove my error. The thought gave me an irrational gleam of hope, and his next words, though I didn't know why at the time, strengthened it.

"Very well. I wonder if you would mind being very quiet in the hall; we've been told there's illness in the next apartment."

The hope wasn't quite enough to sustain me, for as we went down the hall I found myself looking about nervously. Those closed doors had never before seemed so dark and unfriendly. What if I were to knock on one of them and demand that the neighbors help me?—But the neighbors didn't know me, I'd never set eyes on any of them—except the man called Spelvin, whom I had passed once or twice in the hall. No, wait! There was Mrs. Pitman, she might vouch for me.

Instinctively whispering, I said, "Just a moment," and walked firmly down the hall to push the bell of apartment 4-A. The man went half way down the top flight of stairs, and stood there; he had not wanted me to ring that bell, but he couldn't very well stop me. And how silently he moved! This was all wrong, it must be a dream, or—that alternative I was trying not to believe.

Nobody answered the ring. I waited, and rang again, and still nobody came. I was sure I'd heard the radio from those rooms only a few minutes ago.

Or hadn't I?

It did no good to stand gazing at the door. With my head spinning, I rejoined the man on the stairs. On this landing the potted fern which should have been standing on the little iron and tile table had disappeared. If I didn't belong in this house, how did I know the fern should have been there? There were three flights to go down. My feet sounded on the treads, muffled but audible. His did not. *Why?*

Something was stirring in my mind, a story I'd heard, or read—about a girl whose testimony nobody would believe. It was only a vague memory as yet, and we were in the foyer, and the man was pressing Mrs. Ulrichson's bell. Her apartment was the only one on the ground floor, a dark basement lair where I pictured her crouching all day among her machine-lace tidies. In a moment I'd see her. I fairly longed for the sight of her shapeless figure and plucked eyebrows.

I glanced sideways at my companion. His deeply tanned face, with each cheek marked by a vertical furrow, looked set in a weary patience. Strong as my impression of his uncertainty had been, I saw no trace of it now.

The door swung open. From where we stood I could see a corner of the landlady's main room, and I looked there first. I knew that room, and it was unchanged; but this person in the doorway was certainly not Mrs. Ulrichson.

It was a man, tall and bony and stooping, and seemingly made of wavering outlines like a cartoon by George Price. His suit looked as if it had been slept in for several nights, his face twitched unhappily as he saw the man beside me, and wafting gently through the doorway came the unmistakable odor of whisky.

"Where's Mrs. Ulrichson?" I said on a sort of gasp.

There was a moment of silence, during which the landlord's eyes slid past me and seemed to consult the big man. Then he looked at me again. I thought his brown eyes might have been kind if they had not been so dull and—yes, so apprehensive.

"Why," he said, "there's nobody of that name here. Was there something I could do? We got no vacancies."

From behind me the deep voice said quietly, "Mr. Bassett, this young lady seems to think I'm occupying her apartment. She insists that she left only Friday morning, but I told her I'd been in 4-D for two weeks."

Bassett spoke slowly, and seemingly with an effort. "That's right."

His apprehension was directed only in part toward the big man. He had looked startled on his first glimpse of me, but now that expression was fading and its place taken by a more confident wariness. In the face of this impregnable front I felt helpless; but when I spoke that must not show in my voice.

"I know I am right," I said. Yes, that sounded sure enough. "This is El Central, and I moved into 4-D on January fifteenth, and paid my rent for a month in advance. If you've taken over this place in Mrs. Ulrichson's absence, you must have gone over her books. Consult them again, and you'll see that I'm telling the truth."

"I never saw you before," Bassett said with perfect accuracy.

"My name is Cameron Ferris."

"There's no such name on the books," he said, and the queerest look flickered behind his eyes, as if he'd thought of something funny.

"Then," I said firmly, "this is a matter for the police."

He continued to stare at me, and now I could detect nothing at all in his expression. The big man took a hand. He was maddeningly indulgent and patronizing.

"No, not the police, I think. You wouldn't like that."

"And why not?"

"They'd call your bluff," he told me quietly. "They'd question me, and Mr. Bassett here, and find that I have full right to that apartment. They'd ask you where your baggage is; you might describe your possessions, but you couldn't produce them. The matter of the key would be easily disposed of. Possibly you knew someone living here, and had an extra key made for the apartment. You've put on a pretty good act for us, but without proof, the police would break down your story in five minutes."

I said, as levelly as I could, "But supposing I have proof?"

The tall man leaned comfortably against the door jamb. "Really, you interest me," he said. There was amusement in his tone, and a veiled insolence. "If I weren't fascinated by the way you keep this up, I shouldn't listen much longer."

I had a sudden, unwelcome flash of imagination. Suppose he were right, after all, how on earth must I look to him? Either he saw me as a queer character, pitching a tall story for dishonest purposes, or—he thought I was crazy.

There was only one thing to do: somehow to convince myself first. I pushed abruptly past Bassett and went into the landlord's apartment. "I want to sit down," I replied to his startled bleat of protest.

I'd been here only twice before, but this place had not changed. I recognized the tidies over the back of every chair and sofa, and the chromo of a "Yard of Kittens" against the dull tan wallpaper. They looked like long-lost friends to me.

With private astonishment at the sure sound of my voice, I suggested, "You sit down too, and let's talk this over reasonably."

Bassett, although standing quite still, managed to give the impression of fluttering. He looked perfectly miserable, but he lowered himself into a chair. The big man stayed on his feet, gazing down at me. Something had restored his confidence too; I wondered if I had imagined his indecision in my apartment and the hall. If not, I'd had the advantage there—and had let it slip through my fingers.

"I'm quite sincere, you know," I said slowly, "in believing that I belong in the flat upstairs. There are things about it that I couldn't possibly know unless I'd lived there in the past month. Suppose I try to make you see that, before I call the police?"

Unluckily, just then the story in its entirety had come back into my mind. Woollcott had told it as a legend, about a mother and daughter coming to the Paris Exposition, the mother dying in a hotel room and the affair being so completely hushed up that everyone thought the daughter's claims were the ravings of insanity. I knew very well that nothing of the sort had happened in this case, but what stuck in my mind was this: the gendarmes had been utterly incredulous, they had refused to listen to a wild tale which seemed without foundation. You could scarcely blame them.

There was that letter, I remembered with a sudden surge of hope—Merideth's last letter to me, at this address, postmarked February 9. I had my handbag open to produce it before I realized that it had been tucked into the pocket of my lost overnight case. I took a handkerchief out of the bag, and shut it. All my bright ideas were coming back on me like boomerangs.

So, the truth wouldn't serve. "When you moved into 4-D," I said, "surely you changed the newspaper under the drip pan of the stove. Maybe you can tell me what you found beneath it."

"A few crumbs," said the tall man promptly.

I said, "Oh, then you didn't change it. I knew as much. Men wouldn't think of anything like that. Since the original newspaper is still there, I can tell the police—without going into the kitchen—what date was on it, and what's written on the card that I slipped under the paper, only last Friday. I'll tell you, so you won't accuse me of bluffing again. It's a recipe for cheese soufflé, in my own handwriting."

Bassett, who seemed uncomfortable, avoided my eyes. I thought I might have shaken his conviction, but the other was my real opponent. I continued to look at the big man.

His face contracted a very little, and then he smiled and said gently, "They won't find it, I'm afraid. And the date on the newspaper?"

Into the trap I went, headlong. "Last Sunday, February seventh."

"The seventh!" the man said, and glanced at Bassett, shaking his head significantly. "Now, Miss Ferris, I'm sure that the place for you is the hospital."

Maybe he's right, maybe he's right, said the treacherous voice inside me. Aloud, I said, "Nonsense."

"Oh, I don't believe it's anything serious," he said soothingly. ("That's right," Bassett murmured painfully.) The other went on, "Supposing you go away and get a good night's sleep. You'll feel better in the morning."

I turned to the landlord. He didn't look like much of a help: his dead-looking brown hair was disheveled, his eyes were filmed and wavering: but I felt that he was taking only a passive part and might be won over. "Would you show me your registrations?" I said. "There must be some record, or a notation of the date when I paid my rent."

"That will be fine," said the big man unexpectedly.

Bassett's muddy brown eyes flickered; he looked hunted. Then, murmuring something in the nature of a weak protest, he rose and brought out a small ring-backed ledger. That meant the leaves were removable, but—would that fact help me?

I read the roster of the tenants on my floor. 4-A, Mrs. Pitman; 4-B, Mr. and Mrs. H. Johnson, rent paid in advance on February 7; 4-C, G. Spelvin, January 1. 4-D—there it was before my eyes: B. Smithers, February 1.

There was no page for C. Ferris, anywhere in the book. I looked for it twice.

In that moment I would have gone. They had me all but beaten, I'd have been more than thankful to escape from this uneasy nightmare—if there had been any place to run to.

There was sixty-seven cents in my purse. My suitcase was in a stranded bus, thirty miles from San Francisco. I thought of those things, and realized that, with one exception, there wasn't a soul in the city to whom I could appeal. The exception was Mr. Tripp.

I couldn't take it. He'd warned me against living alone, he'd told me I should not leave the country until morning. Maybe he wouldn't say, "I told you so," but he would surely think it—and at the very best he'd be more and more protective and dictatorial, taking for granted that I'd turn to him in trouble. I wasn't letting anything be taken for granted. Rather than that I'd sleep on a bench in the Ferry Building.

Maybe, quite literally, I should have to. I began to fasten my raincoat, with rather unsteady fingers, and the big man watched me with a sort of remote compassion.

I had all but made up my mind to try the girls' club. They knew me there, perhaps they would trust me, even without money or luggage. If they asked any questions, and I explained truthfully, they'd be *certain* to take me to the hospital. Somehow I'd have to invent a plausible story...

It was as near as that.

Then I saw the wastebasket.

It was one of those open wire ones, and half way down in the pile of rubbish, bulging through the meshes, was a crumpled piece of paper in a peculiarly horrible shade of coral pink with white edges. I knew there couldn't be a duplicate in this house of the samples that a printing firm had handed round to the personnel of Caya's. With true Scottish thrift I had brought mine home to use for scratch paper, and on Friday I had pushed under Mrs. Ulrichson's door a half-sheet with these words scribbled on it:

"If my laundry comes, will you put it inside
my door? Shall be away until Monday evening.
Thanks very much.

C. Ferris, 4-D."

As if in despair I stared at the bit of paper, while a wave of good healthy anger took the place of my doubt. The paper, I'd swear, had not been there for two weeks. These two gentlemen were playing games with me.

What was more, they thought they had me thoroughly buffaloed, while right in my hands I had the weapon to defeat them.

"Maybe—maybe you're right," I said dully, and put a hand up to my head. "I'm so tired—I don't know where I could go." The unsteadiness of my legs, when I got up, was quite in character though involuntary. Once more I put on a piteous look, and added, "I suppose I could find a hotel that would take me in, but I haven't any money."

"If that's all, I'll give you a couple of dollars," said the big man, and brought a handful of silver out of his trousers pocket. Mr. Bassett sprang suddenly to life; he hadn't liked this, but he was afraid of the other one.

"That's right, you go away and get some rest," he said in a relieved tone. "It's too bad to see a young girl like you, wandering around."

Without shame I took the money, keeping my head down. "It's still raining," I sighed, "I—I hate to go out in the rain—Oh, my overshoes! I left them in the hall upstairs—if you'd just come up with me to get them—Mr. Smithers, isn't it?" I turned to my chief enemy. "I can't go out without rubbers, in this storm."

Bassett was easy; he fumbled ineffectually and gave way, shaking his head, when I pushed him aside and got to the door.

"Or," I said brightly, "I still have my key. I can go up alone."

The big man said, "Don't trouble. I'll get the overshoes and bring them down. Mr. Bassett will wait here with you."

"Sure," the landlord said hopefully, "you stay with me, Miss."

"How do I know you'll bring them down?" said I, raising my voice a little so that it echoed in the enclosed foyer. I'd show him how crafty these lunatics could be. "You might just get in there and shut the door and never come out, and I'd have to ruin my shoes in the rain and maybe catch cold. I'll come right up with you!"

There was a fine loud ring to those last words, and I saw the tall man's jaw go tight. "Please, hush," he said. "If you disturb the tenants, we'll have to explain to them that you're—not quite right. Very well, come if you must, but be quiet."

I looked cowed, shut my mouth and crept meekly up the stairs behind him. The big window in my living room, I remembered, was closed and the shade was down. In any event, it looked out on the blank rear wall of another building, and the wind and rain were howling outside so that you couldn't hear yourself think. There was a more obvious way to defeat him, but I wanted my victory all to myself.

The man unlocked the door of 4-D, and motioned me in. He was careful to close it behind him, and his voice was very low as he said, "There are your galoshes. Put them on and get going. I want to give you a bit of advice, too; don't try this game again. You haven't a Chinaman's chance of getting away with it."

I dropped the overshoes and faced him. "You still think I'm lying?" I said pathetically, and before he could stop me, turned and darted into the kitchen. He wouldn't risk a struggle; I was banking on that. I flicked on the light and swung around, putting out a hand to raise the window that gave on the light well. He had reached the doorway, and I said in a conversational tone, "I'll yell if you come one step nearer. I can yell bloody murder when I want to, and it'll sound worse than that in this light well."

It was the satisfaction of a lifetime to see that large brute stop short. For the sake of prudence I moved closer to the window, and said, "I'll give you five minutes to put your things in a bag and get out of here. You have more to fear from the police than I have, and you're afraid of noise."

He made one more effort. "For your own sake—"

I snapped, "Get on with it. This is my apartment, and you know it as well as I do. What's more, no matter how many faces you make, last Sunday was the seventh of February."

The man drew a deep breath, folded his arms and leaned against the door frame. He said with a faint smile, "Can you produce the recipe for cheese soufflé?"

"There never was one," I told him sweetly. "I cook by instinct. Do you want me to yell?"

"No," he said mildly, "that's the last thing on earth I want." Once more he seemed to be taking my measure, but I couldn't help seeing that his look was tinged with admiration. "Well, my little scheme didn't work, did it?"

"It never had a chance," I lied cheerfully.

"Would it have been any better if I'd asked you politely to let me borrow your room for one night?"

"Scarcely," said I, giving him the old raised eyebrow.

"Nevertheless, I'm going to beg you to go somewhere else—just for this one evening. Please, Miss Ferris. I give you my word; it's not safe for you to be here."

"The story's getting better," I said. "Is it your idea of safety to turn me out alone in the dark? Somehow I'd prefer that you went."

"No," the man said, "I can't go. I'll make this up to you somehow. I'm sorry it happened, but that stunt of trying to bluff you out was the best I could think of at the moment—and you gave me the cue yourself. You see, we'd thought you were to be away."

"Yes, I know."

"And I wish to heaven you'd stayed away. Would you go now, if I told you all hell might break in this building before the night's out?"

I looked at him in complete incredulity. Why, this was a dream after all; or else the man, and not I, was wacky.

"You don't believe me? I could prove it to you. I will, if you'll shut the window."

"I'll do that when you walk out of here."

The man straightened and unfolded his arms. "You win," he observed unemotionally. "I see you're determined, so there's nothing for me to do but go. This will be a nice little mystery for you to think about all your life—if you live through the night."

A curious sensation played around the back of my neck. "That's a silly sort of threat," I said, "and as soon as you're gone

I can demand an explanation from that man downstairs. He wouldn't be such a—a quavering loon if he weren't scared of you. The threats worked on *him*, I suppose."

"Oh, he doesn't know anything," said B. Smithers lightly. "He's only pinch-hitting for his aunt, Mrs. Ulrichson, while she's away for a few days." His eyes were on my face. "Yes, there is a Mrs. Ulrichson. That worried you, didn't it?—I'm the only one, Miss Ferris, who knows why I had to take over your apartment, to make it look as if I lived here, and who can tell you what kind of hell is going to break loose, and who your neighbors are."

—A nice little mystery, for me to wonder about all my life.—

He couldn't have dangled a more alluring bait than the situation of this insane set-up, nor could he have offered me a neater loophole than was suggested in his next words.

"I could tell you about it in half an hour or less, if you'd consent to listen. No, please—" His hard mouth twitched into a grin, somehow rather disarming. "Please don't flash your eyes at me again. I know you're angry, and you have every right to be. But—when it means not only your own safety, but the lives of two or three others as well—couldn't you gamble thirty minutes?"

"Certainly I deserve some kind of explanation," I said slowly. "You can begin on it, I'll grant you that much—but make it good."

"Thank you." He actually sketched a sardonic bow. "If I might suggest it—you can't be very comfortable there, leaning on the oven. Won't you come into the living room?"

"I think I'll stay right here, by the window."

"For your information," the man said, with the effect of making a concession, "a good scream delivered anywhere in this apartment would ruin all my plans. Your weapons will be just as potent if you're sitting down. And," he added after a moment's wait, "you know—you needn't be afraid of me, personally."

"I'm not," I said, flicking a glance up and down him.

The words actually made him color faintly, under the brown of his skin. He stared at me angrily for a moment, and then the flush receded.

"Atta girl," said B. Smithers, with obvious relief and pleasure.

The queer thing was that I'd spoken the truth, and the insulting intent was only superficial. He looked like the kind of person you'd ask to help you out of a turbulent crowd—competent, impersonal and trustworthy. The crow's feet beside his eyes had been made, and the furrows in his cheeks deepened, by laughter. He was spare and hard in spite of his great size, and though the shabby clothing was obviously his, I felt that he'd look just as comfortable in English tailoring. He was older than I'd thought at first glance; somewhere between thirty-five and forty, judging by the drifts of gray in his dark hair.

"Walk ahead of me, please," I said, and moved slowly after him as he shrugged his shoulders and obeyed. "You'll have to talk fast, Mr. Smithers."

"Please," he said, "not *that* name. I had to use it, because it was on the papers I borrowed to impress Mrs. Ulrichson."

"What papers were those?"

"They made me out to be a private detective," he said, turning in the bright light of the living room to confront me with a grin. "I'm supposed to be collecting evidence on an erring husband."

"On this floor of this apartment house?"

"Sure."

"You wouldn't find him in my place," I said dryly, "and there's a bachelor on one side of me and a youngish couple on the other—with a baby."

"With a *what?*" His eyes blazed suddenly, and the big frame went rigid.

"A baby."

"Keep your voice down!"

"Sorry, I thought you were hard of hearing."

"How do you know they have one?"

"I saw it, and heard it," I said patiently. "Is this the best you can—"

"Skip it," the man said. I couldn't ignore the authority in his voice. "When did you see it?"

"The early part of the week, and what's it to you?"

"A lot. Monday or Tuesday?"

"Tuesday afternoon." His urgency shook my defenses. "A woman was coming up the stairs as I went down—I'd been sent on an errand by the office, and had come home to get my raincoat. I thought she was just visiting here, calling on Mrs. Pitman, perhaps; but on Friday morning, just before I left, I heard the child crying in the next room, in 4-B."

"You're sure it was there?"

"Of course. I looked out the window to make sure, and the same woman came to her window and slammed it down. The crying had stopped by then. That was the only time I'd heard a sound."

"Good Lord!" the big man hissed, and struck his clenched fist into the palm of his other hand. He continued to stare at me, his eyes brilliant. "Maybe there's a chance for us after all."

Then a new thought came into his mind. I could see it steal across his face, and the triumphant expression changing slowly to one of dismay. "But if that's so," he said in a whisper, "if they know you saw it—Miss Ferris, what I said about your being in danger was mostly talk. Now—after this, I'm afraid it's true. You *can't* leave, now."

FOUR

My Own Petard

I SAID, "Changed your mind *again*, Mr. Smithers?" but the effect of this was marred by my involuntary step backward.

"My name's Barney," he said absently, his troubled gaze still on my face. "You might as well have something to call me."

"If you think I—"

"Don't get any ideas into your head. You're nothing to me but an added burden. If you'd had the sense to get out while the going was good, while we were downstairs, you'd have been all right; but now that you've been up here talking to me, there's no way of telling—what might happen to you."

After that hesitation his voice had dropped even lower than before. He was staring right through me now, his mind almost visibly turning this way and that, gauging possibilities even as he spoke.

I was silent. From a personal duel with someone who had inexplicably tried to frighten me out of my room, this had suddenly become a major battle. Maybe I believed him too readily, but when someone tells you you're in danger—in that tone of voice—you generally duck first and ask for proof afterward.

Into that brief silence came an almost imperceptible sound that sent a chill racing up my back. It was the light tap of a fingernail on glass.

The man's head jerked round toward the big window. He froze for a second, and then got into action. "In there!" he commanded in a whisper, jerking open the dressing-room door, "and keep still. Don't show yourself."

The door closed. For all his size, he could move as stealthily as a huge cat, for I could barely hear his progress across the main room. There was a rustle, as if the window shade had been pulled aside, and then a soft exclamation.

I had to see what went on. One step brought me to a point of vantage, the crack of the loosely fitting door on which the wall bed was suspended. The dressing-room was dark, but the outside room was brilliantly lighted.

The shade of my big window had been raised, and the window itself silently pushed up. It was as silently lowered as I reached the crack. A man had come in from the fire escape.

"Have you lost your mind, O'Shea?" Barney demanded in a low voice. "I thought you weren't to appear at all—and then you go right past that window."

The other man was, for the moment, invisible. When he replied it was in a smooth monotone, but a perfectly audible one. There was a curious precision about his speech.

"Appear was meant in the official sense, Barney," he said. "Did you think I could stay away completely? And I have not been seen."

"Where were you?"

"On the roof of the building across the alley in back. I had a view of several familiar shadows on the blinds of that apartment next door. Our friends, Barney, are not quite confident."

"You're telling me. And you smoothed them down by coming up their fire escape?"

"There was no risk in that," said O'Shea blandly. "They have gone."

"Gone! What the—"

"About twenty minutes ago," the suave voice continued (and was interrupted by Barney, saying bitterly, "While I was downstairs!") "—about that time the lights in 4-C went out, and someone raised the shade and looked out. Then a dim light shone, probably from the hall, and they went out—all three of them. They did not come back. They carried one or two small suitcases."

"The hell they did. Nothing else?"

"Nothing."

Barney waited for a moment before replying. His voice when it came was entirely without inflection.

"If this is a double-cross—" he said, and left the sentence hanging in mid-air. The very flatness of his tone made it sound incredibly threatening.

"Oh, not by me, Barney," said the other man. "Not by me. I do not settle my scores by helping an enemy to escape."

There was another brief silence. "Okay, Colly," Barney said at last, "I'm inclined to believe you. But—where did they go?"

"Across the hall, perhaps?"

"That wouldn't do them much good. Out of the building, maybe, while I was in Bassett's apartment; but they can't have taken *it* along, or they'd have been spotted."

"You are sure?" O'Shea inquired.

"Sure. Both ends of the alley and the front door are covered. —Good God, did they get it to another hideout, earlier?—but I know it was there Friday morning—and I'll swear they haven't moved it since I've been here."

Mr. O'Shea disposed of the theory of another hideout. "The boys would have known," he said confidently. All at once his back appeared in my line of vision, the head turned a trifle toward one side of the living room. He seemed to bend an interested gaze on the wall, but nothing was there except a pair of tinted photographs depicting *Cupid Asleep* and *Cupid Awake*.

The only impression I could gather from this rear view was that of an extraordinary supple leanness darkly and cheaply clothed, of a height something above average, and a cap dragged down over close-cut sandy hair. He had moved with a fluid swiftness.

For about half a minute Barney had been giving out with as novel and pungent a bit of swearing as I'd ever heard. Now he let it trail off, and sighed. "I can't go out hunting," he said bitterly, "without removing the last doubt from their minds. They weren't sure I was lying, but if they caught me snooping now, they would be. And a while ago they were right under my nose."

The darkly clothed shoulders lifted in a shrug. "Perhaps they still are," said Colly O'Shea. "We can find out soon enough." He turned and moved silently into the hall, but so close was he to the dressing-room door that I knew when he stopped short. The suave voice was more subdued than ever.

"Since when, Barney, did you take to wearing white rubber overshoes?" he asked gently.

O Lord, I thought, they say criminals always overlook something. In about one minute this O'Shea will begin looking around; I'm trapped here, I'll be caught trying to disguise myself as a bedspring—

"Those are mine," I said, opening the door and stepping out.

One of the men, I think, was angry and the other startled; but they looked at me without the slightest change of expression, and in silence. This sudden front view of Mr. O'Shea was, to say the least, astonishing. He seemed to have no color anywhere in his face, since the sandy eyebrows and lashes were all but invisible, and the impassive eyes of so light a gray as to be almost white. Speechless, we stood face to face.

Well, Cameron, I thought—you were the girl who complained that she never met any unusual men.

"Your mouse?" O'Shea inquired at last. He spoke to Barney, but continued to gaze at me.

With haste Barney forestalled my indignant denial. "No," he said, "she's the real tenant of this apartment. She dropped in a bit earlier than we expected. Miss Ferris, Mr. O'Shea," he added punctiliously.

O'Shea's capped head ducked toward me. "It is a pleasure," he said in a tone that canceled his words. "And you had not meant to tell me she was here?"

"Not if I could help it," said Barney shamelessly. "I hadn't forgotten my promise, Colly, but this couldn't be avoided. By the way, it was Miss Ferris who proved to me that we were on the right track. She saw and heard the child."

O'Shea looked at him quickly. Their gazes locked and held.

"I may add," I said, "that I have no idea of what this is all about."

"May I ask, Miss Ferris," said O'Shea with deadly politeness, "under what circumstances you saw—"

"She said a woman was carrying it upstairs on Tuesday afternoon," Barney put in.

"What did the woman look like?"

"From one glimpse of her," I said wearily, "I can't give a complete description. I had no reason to stare. It seems to me she was medium height, dark, and rather full-faced. But—"

"Gertie," said O'Shea, and nodded slowly. The white eyes held a peculiar gleam. "That should please both you and me, Barney. This girl—" He paused for a moment, and looked full at me. "This is your affair. If they are in the front apartment," he had dismissed me with a gesture and now made one of his fluid movements toward the door, "nothing has been lost."

I suppose I had been hypnotized by the definiteness of Barney's commands, and the taut expectancy of both men as they spoke to each other and to me. Every nerve in my body was tingling, but I simply stood there and watched, pop-eyed, while Barney stepped quietly into the public corridor and laid his ear against the door—not of 4-B, but the one belonging to my bachelor neighbor, Mr. Spelvin.

He shook his head as he returned to my hallway.

"In a moment," O'Shea said imperturbably, "I will have a look from the front fire escape."

Barney gazed at him with narrowed eyes. "They couldn't possibly have *left* it next door?"

"I doubt that, but we can see. The window catches are very simple."

"You're a useful fellow, Colly," Barney said with a grin. "Of course, there's always the chance that we're walking into a trap."

"There is, indeed. I should welcome that, but it might not improve your own chances."

"And you'd rather catch 'em in the act. About fifty-fifty, it seems to me. We'll both go." He caught up the leather jacket and threw it across his shoulders.

With the utmost aplomb, the two gentlemen crossed the room, once more raised shade and window, stepped onto the fire escape and vanished. Since their arrangements had not included me, I was left standing in the hall struggling with a fine case of the screaming meemies.

They moved so fast, and so quietly! They were so businesslike—

And what on earth did it all *mean*? What was I doing here, a speechless witness to this meeting of crooks? The sight of Mr. O'Shea was not reassuring, and he and Barney were hand in glove on some project that took in my neighbors in a peaceful, respectable apartment house. This couldn't be real.

I shook my head violently, to clear it. Yes, it was real. There was the disguised living room, there were my overshoes on the floor, there was the sound of rain drumming on the fire escape. I had walked into the middle of a wild melodrama; but who were the villains?

Whatever happened was to come off tonight. Barney had asked to borrow my room "for one night."

Mr. O'Shea was attempting to settle a score with an enemy.

The baby that I had seen once, and heard once, was somehow important in the matter. I walked thoughtfully into the living room, several improbable ideas jockeying for place in my mind.

When almost ten minutes had passed since the men had left, and not a sound had come from next door, I wondered suddenly why I was standing here waiting for their return, instead of grabbing my rubbers and getting the hell out the front door. Well, no; I needn't wonder. I knew. I would be curious for the rest of my life if I didn't find out what all this was about.

So I put my head out the window and was rewarded by the sight of Mr. O'Shea, drifting like a shadow down the iron ladder which led from the roof. He peered through the window of 4-B, and murmured a few indistinguishable words. At once Barney emerged from the window, and O'Shea, with a side glance at me, remarked in his soft monotone, "Since they may return, I think I shall stay here."

Barney said, "It won't be necessary, Colly."

"Oh, yes. This chance is too good to miss. I helped you on two conditions, and one was that when you had finished I should have my turn."

"You'll get it, never fear, and I'll enjoy watching."

"I shall stay," said O'Shea's colorless lips, "to make sure of that." He bent double and slid through the open section of the bay window.

In another moment the big man was beside me, and my window was again closed and shaded against the wet darkness. Deliberately he peeled off the damp leather coat and hung it in the closet; returning to the living room, he looked at me, and abruptly chuckled.

"Any questions, Miss Ferris?" he offered politely.

"If you think half an hour's explanation will cover everything, you'll have to begin pretty soon," I said.

"Oh, that," he said slowly. "That bargain is off."

"What do you mean by that?"

"I mean that conditions have changed, and we have lots of time."

"No," I said, "things aren't quite the same. You didn't want me to see your visitor, did you? But I did."

"I didn't want him to see *you*."

Seemed to me it worked both ways, but I said, "Why not? Is he the source of that danger you've been trying to frighten me with?"

"Not the same one; another. A potential one."

"And you and he are working together."

"For the present," said the big man imperturbably, "we are."

I spread a hand, palm upward. "And after admitting that, you think I can stay here quietly and listen to you telling lies as fast as you can think them up?"

"I think you'll stay here, yes. But you'll be hearing the truth."

"That's open to doubt, Mr. Barney," I said. "Before that creature turned up at the window, you'd started some kind of an explanation. May I ask if it was planned to include him?"

Once more he gave me that faint, rueful smile. "This is a game of Truth? Very well; no, it wasn't. And, by the way—no Mister. Just Barney."

"I don't care what your name is. How can you expect me to take you on trust—now?"

Barney put both hands on the back of a straight chair, and rocked it back and forth on its hind legs. "I have no right to expect that," he said thoughtfully, "but I imagine you will—just because you've stayed in the game this far. Whether you meant to or not, you've placed a bet on my side."

"I certainly didn't—"

"Wait a minute." The level eyes held me silent. "Believe it or not, this situation hurts me worse than it does you. It was a shock for you to come in your own door and see me here, but that was nothing to the way I felt when I realized who you were. And when I failed to bluff you out, I *asked* you to leave. You wouldn't. That refusal put you into this affair, up to the neck."

He was right, of course. I'd had two chances to go, but curiosity and stubbornness had kept me here.

"Neither of us can afford to give way," he added. "We're in it together, though not by choice. Come on," and again he flashed that strangely appealing grin, "can't we arrange a working truce?"

I stood gazing at him, considering what he said in the light of reason. Reason told me I'd be more than foolhardy if I agreed to spend an unspecified portion of the coming night with a stranger; my reputation at the very least would be jeopardized, possibly a great deal more. Roger cared for my reputation. Did I want to risk losing his approval?

All my conscious, sensible self warned me of danger, reminded me of the serpent-like ally within call in the next apartment, told me that after all I hadn't been built for the role of adventurer.

What I really listened to was the small voice of the opposition.

—"Nobody will ever know—" it said. "—He told you that it was unsafe for you to leave, and you believed him.—Choose the known evil, the visible one.—You can take care of yourself.—"

"All right," I said abruptly, "for the time being. I suppose I've little choice."

"You're quite right to reserve your judgment," he said, meeting my eyes. "I hope you won't feel that way long. Now that we've settled that much, won't you take off your coat and sit down?"

Keeping my glance warily on his, I unfastened my slicker and topcoat and gave them into his outstretched hands. Had he known instinctively that I'd refuse an offer of help? How much of his action was instinct, and how much extraordinarily acute design?

There was, for instance, the matter of his voice and intonation. As he spoke to the O'Shea creature, he'd sounded hard as nails; with the landlord he managed to convey a threat and a warning under the cool straightforwardness of his tone. With me, nothing was apparent but courtesy, and what I could have sworn was innate fineness.

Since he could change so easily, which of these manners was the true one?

I sat down in the farther corner of the chesterfield, watching him narrowly. He made as if to seat himself beside me, was stopped short by my look, and stood reflecting for a moment; a quick glance considered and rejected the dubious comfort of the occasional chair. Then, completing an expressive bit of pantomime, he picked up from the table a pile of folded newspapers, and placed it in the middle of the chesterfield.

"A sword," he said gravely, gave the papers a satisfied pat, and lowered himself into the other corner.

A chuckle almost caught me unawares. It wasn't fair that he should have a taste for small absurdities.

He reached a long arm for the ashtray. "Will you have a cigarette, Miss Ferris? Really, they're not doped. I'll bet you need one."

"What makes you think I smoke?" I inquired coldly.

"Circumstantial evidence," said Barney with an unabashed grin.

"Of course. You pawed over all my possessions before you hid them." He continued to hold out the cigarettes, and half against my better judgment I took one. He'd been quite right; I needed it.

With ineffable modesty he replied to my remark. "When I came to the stuff in the chest of drawers, of course I closed my eyes. You are dealing with a perfect gent."

—Keep your face straight, Cameron! I thought. Remember your practice-teaching, and how those young hellions knew they could get away with anything if they could make you laugh first.

I leaned back after accepting the proffered light, and asked, "What did the perfect gent do with his hostess's suitcases and furnishings?"

He had crossed his knees and was looking comfortable and settled.—Now, his manner indicated, we're off on a friendly conversation.

"In the kitchen," he said, "there is a tall stepladder. In the hall ceiling there is a sort of trapdoor—scuttle hole, they call it—that you climb through to get to the electric wiring. Add these: total, one neat temporary hiding place. If you'd come back tomorrow, as we expected, you'd have found your belongings all back in place. There'd have been no signs that I'd ever been here." He took a puff on his cigarette, and thoughtfully quoted my initials. "A. C. F. What's the A. stand for?"

—Really, I thought, is this a social call?—and heard myself answer, "Agnes."

"Nobody calls you that, I should imagine. You spoke of yourself as Cameron; that's pleasant."

"So glad you approve," I said. "Now that that's settled, do you mind telling me the meaning of all this?"

"Oh," said Barney, as if recalled from an interesting train of thought. "You mean my having moved in here, and tried to make it look like home? But I had to have some place to entertain my friends!" There was mockery behind his innocent look.

"Your friends; h'm. Do they include that albino snake next door?"

"I gather that Colly didn't appeal to you."

"Well," I said, "when Eduardo Ciannelli turns up in a movie, nobody thinks he's there for any good purpose. Your Mr. O'Shea doesn't look like him, but—the impression is there."

Barney said, "He's not entirely sinister, you know. There's been education there, at some time—that careful speech is peculiar to him. He's helped me to get here, too, at considerable risk to himself. By the way, it would be kind of you if—well, the fact is, Colly prefers not to appear in this case, except privately. He means to do his part, and then—just disappear. It's owing to him, I think."

"And who is he?"

Instead of answering, the big man chuckled again. "The first time I knew he was out—out west here," he corrected himself hastily as if he'd made a slip—"was at the 'Thirty-nine Fair. I was going around the Fine Arts Building, and saw him; how come he'd got in there, I certainly couldn't tell you. Anyway, he was studying the Dali."

Fascinated in spite of myself, I said, "Not *Boiled Beans and Soft Construction*?"

You may have seen that remarkable painting. As I remember, the background consists of a landscape strewn with incongruous bits of bric-a-brac, and trees with sewing machines hung in the branches. The foreground, which nobody could forget if he tried, is occupied by a large human figure happily engaged in tearing itself limb from limb.

"Yes," said Barney. "He was spellbound in front of it."

"What did he think of it?" I inquired.

"I didn't ask him. One does not slap Colly on the back when he's not aware of one's presence, so I came away. He was just standing there, looking at it."

I considered this vision, and could not restrain a grin.

"Well, thank heaven," said Barney piously, "you are human after all. Do you know that's the first time I knew you could smile?—Seems as if that picture made Colly a little nervous about art in general. He's been looking narrowly at the walls of these apartments."

"I saw him," I said, putting out my cigarette. "But what has that to do with you, and my bags being hidden, and the Johnsons' baby?"

Barney waited a moment as if coming to a decision. Then he looked full at me, his light blue eyes cold and remote. "The Johnsons' baby," he said, "is little Melissa Cleveland, who was kidnapped from her home on Pacific Avenue, last Tuesday morning."

He shut his mouth with a snap, and waited for that to sink in.

"*What?* But—but nobody's baby has been kidnapped. It would have been in the papers."

"Not in this case. The people who took her did a slick job, so slick that their very competence was a warning. You remember the de Tristan case, and how clumsy that kidnapper was? There was none of that this time, and when these people threatened that at the first movement of the police or the F.B.I., at the first hint of publicity, the child would die—the parents believed them."

This sudden change of pace left me breathless. He'd succeeded in making me laugh, and probably figured that I'd be more malleable from now on; so, it was time to get down to business. His voice had taken on the flat certainty of a police officer's verbal report.

It carried some of the same conviction, for I felt no doubt that a baby had actually been stolen.

"The parents let themselves be bluffed?" I said, with the hint of scorn all too easy for those who have never been in such a hideous position.

Barney looked at the carpet. "I think they were right," he said. "They didn't make the mistake of underrating their opponent."

I couldn't make out what was behind the reserve in his voice.

"But what was there—what made them think—"

"You might as well know what we're up against," he said. "I'll start with last Tuesday morning, though the story begins a long way back of that; but it came out in the open on Tuesday—Lord," he added in a whisper, "six days of it!"

"Well?" I said, after a wait.

"Well. It was like this."

He began to talk. As one brusque, unemotional sentence followed another, slowly the appalling picture became clear.

...It was like this. In San Francisco there was a man named Walter Cleveland, a wealthy and prominent man who was managing editor of the *Eagle*, an evening newspaper. For several months the paper had been carrying on a crusade against an enemy. There had been vague threats of retaliation made, but they didn't mention Cleveland or his family; then the enemy struck, and the manner of the blow made it plain that this crime had been carefully planned—perhaps for weeks in advance...

"Why didn't they go and sock the enemy?" I put in here.

"They don't know who he is," said Barney briefly.

...The Clevelands, he said, lived in a big, plain, old-fashioned home out on Pacific Avenue. Their servants had been with them for many years, and were undoubtedly loyal to the Clevelands. The one member of the household who received not only loyalty but worship was the eleven-month-old baby, Melissa.

There was one employee newer than the rest: Patsy Gavin, a trained nurse who had full care of the child. Personally, Barney said, he was as sure of her as of the rest; he'd known her from her probationer days—had, in fact, recommended her for the position.

The household, though a wealthy one, was industrious, and clocks could have been set by the regularity of its habits. Mr. Cleveland went to work early; his wife, who was on numerous charitable committees and took them seriously, usually drove away in her own car soon after nine o'clock.

There was a three-car garage behind the house, set rather far back on the property. The doors were left open after the master's and mistress's cars had gone; the garage was in plain sight from the kitchen, where Adams, the old chauffeur, habitually went for a mid-morning cup of coffee. He had kept it in sight on Tuesday morning. He and the cook had watched Patsy Gavin, pretty and trim in her nurse's hat and cape of dark blue lined with scarlet, carrying the little Melissa out to the garage where the perambulator was kept. This morning outing was also habitual. The baby, Barney said, was an appealing little creature, friendlier than most; she would go to anyone who held out his arms.

Miss Gavin disappeared into the garage. A minute or so later an automobile horn sounded in the street, and she came to the door and waved. At this distance, only her gay costume identified her positively. Adams thought that one of her young men friends had dropped by for a brief visit, for she went down the drive toward the street, her head bent over the baby in her arms.

That was the last sight anyone had of Melissa Cleveland. The upstairs maid saw the woman in the nurse's cape getting into a dark sedan—a medium-priced car like thousands of others—speaking to the man behind the wheel, and settling herself in comfort as they drove off. It all looked very normal and casual. Nobody had an idea that anything was wrong until Adams returned to the garage, fifteen minutes later.

He saw that a rear window had been forced; and he found Patsy Gavin sick and dizzy, just recovering from a rabbit punch which had left her unconscious. She had been attacked the minute she stepped inside the door, and the only impression she retained was of "seeing herself in a long mirror." The woman who had impersonated her had been prepared in advance with a duplicate of Miss Gavin's uniform. That, of course, pointed to a careful study of the household and its routine, which must have called for weeks of preparation.

It was so slick and cool as to be almost foolproof. The lost quarter of an hour gave the criminals a chance to disappear without leaving a single clue—except the inevitable kidnap note.

The note, found in the garage, was the more terrifying because it was so businesslike. It was printed in purple ink from rubber-stamp letters, the sort that are sold in sets by

Woolworth's and the stationers. The wording was brief and definite. In effect, it said that if one word were spoken to police, Federal agents, newspapers or radio, the baby would die at once. Instructions would follow. If the Clevelands were willing to negotiate, a certain advertisement should be placed in the Personal column of the *Eagle.*

The servants, who read the note first, kept their heads. They didn't touch the paper (a useless precaution, since it proved to be devoid of fingerprints) and they notified no one but the parents. Mr. and Mrs. Cleveland were, of course, nearly crazed with grief and terror. The editor, thinking that he recognized the hand of his unknown and terribly capable enemy, decided to obey these dictates but to fight with his own weapons.

There was more to it than just rescuing the child, Barney said with a momentary somber gaze at me. The enemy had been forced into this move by a long chain of circumstances. He was risking his own discovery and punishment for other crimes—if he should be caught; but that discovery had, through the *Eagle,* seemed imminent at any rate, and now he had pulled a winning trump out of the deck by getting possession of the child and bargaining with her life.

It was a diabolically clever move, which took danger into account but turned it to an advantage. The Clevelands could fight, but all the obvious weapons were denied them. They might, without the help of the police, attempt to trace a dark Chevrolet sedan whose number nobody had noticed, or the purchase of a nurse's cape and hat or the materials for a facsimile, or a pair of gloves with purple ink on the fingers. They might, in utter secrecy, attempt to comb every mountain cabin in the Sierras and every house in any one of a dozen cities; but these impossibilities could not even be considered.

Conversely, they might pursue the search, already begun, for the anonymous enemy. If they should do so, their baby's life would not be worth a plugged nickel. In his own territory, the enemy would detect any signs of investigation…

"So," I said, "they did nothing?"

Barney turned on me one of those sober glances, focused on a point somewhere behind me. "They did plenty," he said. "Walter Cleveland went to every other newspaper in town and told them what had happened."

"He called that keeping the affair secret?"

"You don't know newspapers. If they agree to keep still, they'd make a clam look gabby. And, since they were naturally anxious to help, he got two or three of the best crime reporters on each paper to work with him."

"You among 'em, do I gather?"

"Well, no, I'm here in another capacity." Barney got up and made a slow, meditative circle of the room. I had been spellbound—and well he knew it—by the smooth and circumstantial story just finished, but now he seemed to feel I should be satisfied.

And, of course, that was only one small part of it. My breath quickened inexplicably as I came out, rather sharply, with the obvious question.

"And who are *you?*"

FIVE

Eat with the Devil

HIS HEAD WAS AVERTED, but in the cheek nearer me I could see the vertical furrow deepening as if he smiled. I had time to think again what an utterly unknown quantity I was faced with: a man who had lied to me and tried his best to make me believe I was crazy, whose story would be supported only by his word. Listen I might, with an interest nobody could help, but could I let myself give way to instinctive belief and—trust? There was a proverb about that, or a bit from W. Shakespeare; it kept jigging in my head, something about the need of a long spoon for those who would eat—

"Who am I?" Barney repeated thoughtfully. "If I tell you the exact truth, you may not like it."

"Give it a try."

"I'm a fruit farmer," he said with an owlish look.

At least five bright rejoinders at once suggested themselves. I think I deserve credit for replying only, "Oh, I see."

"Do you? Well, what's the matter, doesn't it seem likely?"

"Likely as anything else, I suppose. From your looks you might be a mounted policeman, or a wrestler, or—a crook."

"Thank you," the man said gravely. "What I look like doesn't matter. I've known Walter Cleveland for some years."

"And that capacity you spoke of?"

He grinned again. "I represent the sapper division, the rear-guard action; it's my job only because I haven't been around here much in the last ten years, and there's a good chance of my staying unrecognized. And—until you came, I was the leader of a forlorn-hope party."

"Until I came. You mean you hadn't known the baby was here?"

"I've been here since Friday afternoon, keeping the closest possible watch on your next-door neighbors. In that time there hasn't been the slightest indication that they ever so much as *saw* a small child. I thought I was watching an empty rat-hole, but it was the only lead we had."

"I don't see how a kidnapped baby could be kept here, in an ordinary apartment house like El Central."

"Not so ordinary," the man said with a peculiar twinkle in his eye. "It would have been safe enough, except for one thing. Don't you see? With no publicity of any kind, the kidnappers could work the purloined-letter stunt, keeping a child—probably drugged so it wouldn't make them conspicuous—right in town, under the noses of the pursuers. It might have worked perfectly, except for the one thing they hadn't counted on."

"You, I suppose."

"We-e-ell—yes," he admitted, in a very fair imitation of Charlie McCarthy. "Once upon a time, as you guessed, I used to be a cop."

"Shucks," I murmured, "I hoped it was a wrestler."

"Wouldn't football do as a substitute?" he inquired anxiously. "I was a fairly good tackle once. If I knew you better, Miss Ferris, I would show you my biceps."

Curse the man, he made me laugh in spite of myself; and, common sense told me, that wouldn't do. With every involuntary smile, every crosscurrent of sympathy between our minds, my guard was being insensibly relaxed. I fought, but I felt it slipping.

"We can skip that," I said. "Go on from there."

"I didn't care much for the police force as a life job," he said, "but I made some useful friends."

"Don't tell me O'Shea was on the force!"

I remembered that cold flat face with its white eyes, and was once more on guard.

"No, no. Quite the—well, as I was saying, we figured that with my peculiar background I might be able to work from within.

"I could, because of an amazing stroke of luck. It was coming to us, because it was the first one we'd had. All Tuesday and Wednesday I nosed around on the Embarcadero, and the lower reaches of Pacific and Broadway, and the cafes south of the Slot. There were a few people down there who owed me a good turn. Never mind how I ran across Colly, or how he got to know what I wanted; but we met privately on Wednesday night.

"He has excellent reasons for wanting to stay out of sight in this affair, but he had an even stronger reason for taking part in it. Seems there's a gentleman named Jay Ruber, who has a girlfriend called Gertie. Gertie has a brother, Fingers Lossert—a black-browed little fellow, with a short nose." He waited expectantly.

"Is that supposed to mean anything to me?"

"Perhaps not. Maybe you've never seen him—Those three had done Colly some dirt, it seemed, and he didn't take it in a Christian spirit. He was eager to get something on them, and with that end in view, he'd been quietly keeping an eye on the three.

"Things get around, among his friends. They wouldn't dream of telling these things to the police, they'd spit in the eye of a Fed, and they have no love for reporters; but Colly knew something, and when he was assured he could trust me, he gave out with his story.

"It was known, somehow, that Jay and Fingers and Gertie were planning some big job, and Colly was interested. They'd never let their friends know, incidentally, what it was to be, but he found out where Fingers had holed up, right after Christmas. It was a room on the fourth floor of this building.

A face, dimly seen at the time, came back into my memory. "Spelvin?" I said incredulously.

"Yes. Didn't you ever wonder about him?"

"I—well, I did think it might be funny if his name were *George* Spelvin. And yet, there might be people who are really called that."

"He isn't. He—or someone who was laughing up his sleeve—picked out that name as a variant on John Smith or Richard Roe. I suppose they have their right to a bit of quiet amusement on the side."

"But—they're all so respectable here! They mind their own business, and nobody goes in for noisy parties."

He was laughing at me openly, but I was too puzzled to resent it. "Didn't you ever take a look at your neighbors? How come you chose Mrs. Pitman to appeal to, earlier tonight?"

The feeling that I was being dense bothered me. "Because she's the only one of my neighbors I've ever spoken to. We met on the roof hanging out our wash."

"Don't tell me she does her own laundry?"

"Well, it was mostly chiffon panties, apricot and nile green, with lace. She seems to be well off; she had on a pair of diamond bracelets that looked—"

The sentence faltered as a wild idea came into my head. I stared at him, frowning.

"Do you want it straight?" he said soberly, but with laughter in his eyes. "Very well. Mrs. Pitman wouldn't open her door to anyone after nine o'clock at night. She's the mistress of one of the town's most prominent businessmen. Everybody suspects it, but she wouldn't want him caught in the act."

My expression must have been a study, for he grinned more broadly. "That's why Mrs. Ulrichson and Bassett both believed me, when I told 'em I was after someone's husband. They didn't want to let me up here, but my borrowed credentials were too good, and they were scared. I promised to hush it up if they'd cooperate, but to raise a howl if they didn't. These landlords are anxious to look respectable, no matter how much they know about their tenants—and they try not to know too much."

"These landlords!" I tried not to gasp and splutter, but it was hard. "*Then—all* the other tenants are—They want to look respectable. That's why she came down on the rent..."

"Uh-huh," said Barney, indulgently amused. "Now you get it."

"Good grief," I added faintly, "of course, you must have thought I—all you knew about C. Ferris was the name—" Horrified laughter threatened to overcome me.

"'Making som mistakes, netcheral,'" he murmured diffidently.

"Oh, don't apologize." I had to give way. "It's the funniest thing that's ever happened to me. I thought Roger was crazy when he warned me."

"Who's Roger?" The question was casual.

"A man at my office," I said; and a disloyalty of which I was immediately ashamed made me add, "He tells you the plots of movies."

"He knows this apartment house?"

"Oh, no. He was just anxious about my living alone, and I swore the neighborhood was pure as a lily!"

"Probably most of it is. The houses to the north and south may be straight enough. How'd you happen to pick this one?"

"Chance and a low rent." My voice was still quivering. "But surely Mrs. Ulrichson isn't so broad-minded that she'd harbor criminals?"

"No," said Barney, and all at once the amusement left his face. "We'll get back to it now. I took Colly into my confidence about the kidnapping. He said it might be the job Jay and Gertie were planning. He had a hunch that there was someone else involved, who was keeping out of sight, but that wasn't certain. The job could have been all their own idea; it sounded like the way they work together. It seemed like a hot lead. As soon as Colly gave me the tip, we managed to plant some of the newspaper men in the adjoining buildings; and I, as the stranger with handy police connections, got in here.

"But I couldn't just walk in on Jay and Gertie. If I alarmed them—well, you remember the threat they left behind. We'd promised Walter not to take any risks. Poor devil, he's half off his rocker from thinking about the baby."

"But—how long have you been here?"

"Made the arrangements Thursday night. I'd scarcely hoped to get on this floor, but—under pressure—Mrs. Ulrichson admitted that the lady in 4-D was to be away for the weekend. She thought maybe she could fix it up with you if you came back early; then on Friday she called me to say it would be all right, you were staying till Monday. What made you come back?"

"A leaky roof. Go on—what about her?" He was making me urge him for information. I wondered how much he would have liked to suppress.

He moistened his lips, looking at me over his shoulder. "She met with—an accident," he said.

"What happened?" I said.

"You didn't hear anything about it? Look at this."

Barney flipped through the newspapers that were piled between us on the chesterfield. "Here," he said, pulling out a copy of the *Eagle,* dated February 12, and opening it to an inside page.

I followed his pointing finger. Under the heading, "Freak Fall Injures Woman," I saw the name of Mrs. Minnie Ulrichson, and the address of El Central.

"—in emergency hospital with a possible fractured skull," the item read. "No one witnessed the fall, though a bent stair-rod and a heel torn from a shoe seem to indicate that the woman had tripped while going downstairs. Miss Rose Delage, a tenant, returning to her third-floor apartment at noon, found Mrs. Ulrichson unconscious. A hall table beside her had been displaced. The woman's head injury was presumably caused by a heavy potted plant jarred from the table by the force of her fall.

"According to Dr. J. J. Warfield of the hospital staff, Mrs. Ulrichson's condition is critical.

"This is the third household accident to occur—"

The rest was irrelevant. I glanced up with knitted brows, and met Barney's eyes. He said, "I'll bet anything that even if she recovers she won't know what—or who—struck her."

"Were you here when that happened?"

"No. It was after I talked to her and before I moved in."

"Do you think it was—deliberate?"

He shrugged. "I know what I *think*, but there's nothing to prove her fall wasn't accidental."

"Don't the police investigate those accidents?"

"They did in this case, but not thoroughly. Maybe when they came round to ask, the Johnsons didn't answer the bell. Anyway, the woman next door told them whom to notify, and they got hold of the nephew. He came right over. He was in possession—and all of a flutter—when I got back here with my bags; so of course I had to pitch my detective yarn all over again, and scare him a bit into the bargain. That's when we took your sheet out of the ledger, just as a precaution."

"You must have scared him thoroughly," I said. "He backed you up like a good one."

"Yes. He did, didn't he?" said Barney thoughtfully. "Well," he went on after a moment, "it was too bad that poor old Ma had to be bopped, but it helped me, in a way. I made myself believe that two mights added up to a must. Jay and his friends might be the criminals, she might have seen the baby that morning, and had to be silenced. This *must* be the right track—and still there was no proof.

"And then you arrived, and casually let drop the one thing I needed. —That bit of knowledge puts you in danger, as sure as if you'd picked up a time bomb."

The jump my heart gave, the sudden crisping of my nerves, told me something beyond doubt. In emotion, if not in judgment, I believed this story.

"Those people didn't see me, did they?"

"Don't be too sure," said Barney grimly. "I don't believe they knew what we said to each other, nor why we went downstairs. You might have returned for something you'd forgotten when you moved—people move often and suddenly from these apartments. But don't forget that while we were on the first floor they left that room. We didn't meet them in the halls, so I'll bet they were hidden somewhere, and saw us come up again."

He leaned forward. "They had reason to feel a bit nervous about me already. How would they have figured it if you—the one remaining witness—talked to me for a few minutes and then went away? Maybe you'd given them away, maybe you hadn't, maybe I wasn't after them at all—but in any case it would pay them to see that you talked to nobody else. And don't think they wouldn't have managed it. There are plenty of dark alleys around here."

I had a vivid picture of that in my mind, and as I studied it my insides curled up like the leaf of a sensitive plant. Neighbors who were so anxious for privacy that without a second thought they'd leave you in an alley with a fractured skull—

So anxious for their privacy that when I returned they left their apartment for another point of greater advantage—

"Look here," I said, frowning, "isn't it possible that—that I've ruined all your plans already, just by turning up? Maybe I deserve to be hit over the head!"

Barney looked around at me, slowly; and slowly he began to grin. "Well, blow me down," he said. "I do believe you're on our side."

It was almost with a feeling of relief that I thought, Judgment be hanged! Emotion had the upper hand from the minute when I'd begun to accept Barney at face value, though I couldn't have told you when that happened.

Emotion had been the stronger power, all along. Without my own volition I had taken a momentous step forward. At the beginning, I hadn't meant to settle down amicably with this stranger; now, disturbingly, the choice had been taken out of my hands. I believed in him, and I—oh, put it into words; I liked him.

No use now to quote the line about eating with the devil. At sight of the dish of excitement he offered, I'd discarded my long spoon.

"Who wouldn't be?" I said on a deep breath.

He continued to gaze at me, and the grin faded to an enigmatic half smile. What was behind it? Triumph, admiration, or something I didn't dare name?

Though neither of us moved, I felt as if I'd held out a hand and he had taken it in a strong clasp.

There was a curious glow behind the ice blue of his eyes. I tried to look away, and found unexpectedly that until he released me I could not.

"I don't know what I can do to help," I added rather shakily.

"Do nothing," he said with emphasis, "and don't get into danger."

Now that his look was averted, I came to myself. (Do rabbits really get hypnotized?) "But what are you supposed to be doing here?"

He turned abruptly, and I all but shrank back at sight of the white fire in his face. "Haven't you got that yet? What do you think I'm doing? I'm waiting for a crisis. The ransom is to be paid tonight. Tonight!"

"And you'll get—" my throat went suddenly dry—"they'll return the—"

"The baby?" said Barney remotely. "If anything goes wrong the baby will be dead by morning."

...He could sit here, I learned, because for a time there was nothing else to do. To keep as free as possible from direct suspicion, he had to sit tight, and let the newspaper men, who had every exit from the building under an unobtrusive guard, take over the surveillance of the criminals. Though the three had escaped from his immediate observation, they must still be in the building; if they should leave, a signal would come from below.

If no one signaled to him, his part of the job was finished; but in any event, he must keep out of sight and look innocent.

"I feel so damned ineffectual," he said with a rueful chuckle, "that I've had to remind myself of all the long sieges in history. But you see, I feel certain, from things I've seen and heard, that the kidnapping plot has headquarters in this building; I managed to learn that much from what your neighbors said to each other. There were references to certain times that were too exact for coincidence."

"You can't hear people talking through these walls."

"No," Barney said, "but the ceilings are thinner." He saw my incredulous look, and grinned. "Did you ever open that scuttle hole in the hall ceiling?"

"Where you hid my things? No, why should I?"

"You come here," he said, "and I'll show you something."

The ladder he brought from the kitchen was an unusually tall one. He had found it, said Barney calmly, in the staircase enclosure which led from the outside corridor to the roof, and had brought it into my kitchen late on Friday night. Even kidnappers, he figured, had to sleep sometimes—though he'd been in mortal terror that the creaking board outside their door would arouse them. You couldn't pass that door without making a bit of noise, but that worked both ways since it had served to advise him of all their comings and goings.

"By George," he added, pausing in the act of setting up the ladder, "the stairway to the roof—that's where they must have hidden while you and I went past."

"But where did they go then, onto the roof? It was raining pitchforks while we were arguing downstairs."

He shook his head. "The roof wouldn't do them any good. They'd have had to get down somehow, and the boys would have spotted them. No, I think they went down the regular stairs as soon as we were shut in here. No telling for sure where they are now, but I have a fairly good idea.

"Well, look, Cameron—I beg your pardon, Miss Ferris."

He had raised the square of boards which covered the hole in the hall ceiling. Obediently I clambered up the ladder and took the flashlight he handed me, swinging its powerful beam about the enclosed space under the flat roof.

Except for a narrow platform around the scuttle hole, the rafters were uncovered. They stretched away as far as sight could penetrate into the dusty dimness: a ribbing of rough two-by-fours, separated by rectangular canyons of lath and plaster, crossed here and there by a network of electric wiring. This space extended across the entire top of the building.

"All I had to do was crawl across those," said Barney, standing below me on the ladder. Instinctively he spoke in a whisper. "I had to be quiet, of course; but the wires led me right where I wanted to go, over the ceiling of 4-B. I heard some interesting talk."

I flashed the light behind me and saw my suitcases and furnishings, neatly stacked on the platform. It gave me an odd and unpleasant feeling, as if there stood all that was mortal of Cameron Ferris.

Even the page from the landlady's ledger, I found later, was hidden in this raftered space. All that remained to prove my existence—

I gave back the flashlight and descended the ladder, rather quickly. Barney had to go up and replace the square of boards, which lifted easily and could be fitted into the hole from below.

He put the ladder in the kitchen, too, murmuring, "Might as well clean up as we go." It was a great unwieldy thing, but he handled it like a yardstick.

"There," he added, facing me and dusting off his hands, "you see the extra advantage of this apartment. Jay and Fingers and the woman chatted freely, since they didn't know anyone could get to a point above them."

"You actually heard them discussing—"

"Well, they didn't say, 'What about the baby we kidnapped from the Cleveland home at ten last Tuesday morning?' But they talked about El Cerrito traffic cops, and speed on the Bay Bridge, and timing. There was one thing I heard—I'm not certain to whom they were referring: the woman said, 'He'll meet you there if he can, but if he's not there by four you'll come back here. It won't take more than half an hour, that time of night.'"

And that, said Barney, could be nothing but a discussion of the ransom plans.

I went back to the living room and sat down, watching the big man as he prowled restlessly back and forth. It was astonishing how freely he talked—almost as if he thought it important that I should be in possession of all these details. I wondered, rather uneasily, if he expected to be in danger himself and wanted me well primed with this story—in case he didn't come back.

No, that couldn't be it. He was talking, I realized suddenly, because of a growing tension. Forced against his inclination to stay quiet and out of sight, he found inaction almost unbearable. It eased him to tell the story to a raptly listening outsider. Anyone else would have done as well.

He'd stop sometimes, and gaze unseeingly at me. It was in those minutes of silence that I recaptured a vivid sense of our surroundings: the two of us, strangers, shut up together in a box suspended high above the gradually slackening motion of the city. Outside, the storm had fallen into a period of comparative quiet. The waterfall roar of rain had diminished, but a wind was coming in fitful gusts, now and then flinging a handful of drops against the window.

But when Barney was speaking I forgot the strangeness and the dreariness. We were in direct communication, and I was caught up by his surcharged vitality.

"—I like talking to you," he interjected into his story at one point. There was a hint of surprise in his tone. I knew, though, why he felt that way; after years of practice, I really am a good listener.

And the pattern was growing. Before long it would be complete.

Midnight; quarter past midnight. There would be some time to wait, as yet, before Barney could expect his signal from below, before Mr. Walter Cleveland would set out from his Pacific Avenue home on a torturing errand.

SIX

Follow My Leader

THERE HAD BEEN more notes from the kidnappers: three in all, counting the original. The first had outlined how the parents were to announce themselves as willing to negotiate. The second, more elaborate, was presented in a different medium, that of words and letters clipped from newspaper columns, but signed by a single initial—C—in the same rubber-stamp letter and purple ink. This one specified the ransom demand, fifty thousand dollars in untraceable small bills.

It asked for something else, too, Barney said cryptically; something that pointed directly to the unknown enemy, and by a hideous irony, the one thing that could not be produced. He stumbled a little on this part, and chose his words carefully. There was, it seemed, an ethical problem involved—or would have been if Mr. Cleveland had been forced to make a choice between saving the baby's life and—something else.

I had my mouth open to ask a question, but he forestalled me with a silencing gesture. The third note, he said, had come on Saturday. It instructed Mr. Cleveland to drive, alone and with nobody following him, to a point in the East Bay. He was to arrive at this specified landmark—on San Pablo Avenue, the arterial to the north—at 3:30 on Monday morning; to turn off the highway onto a stretch of boulevard which ran for five miles through country property, outside the jurisdiction of city police; and to drive slowly up and down those five miles until someone by the road should signal him to stop. This would occur at some time within an hour after his arrival.

It was, I could see, a plan which again plucked the maximum of safety from the obvious danger in which the kidnappers' act had placed them. At three o'clock on a February morning, they would be free from casual observation, and even if the help of the police had secretly been enlisted, it would be difficult to patrol that five miles of road and meadow land without giving the kidnappers warning.

Mr. Cleveland meant to obey these orders to the letter—except that he would have to produce a substitute for the object which was "C's" additional demand.

But, said Barney, there were the times which he had heard mentioned by the three in the next apartment; they coincided so exactly as to leave little room for error. If Jay Ruber and his moll, and Fingers Lossert, went through with the rendezvous according to plan, and if they should escape afterward, they could always be picked up.

"With Mr. O'Shea's help?" I put in.

"Possibly."

"Just how far do you trust him?" I said. "You made some remark about a double-cross."

Barney appeared to muse. "Under ordinary conditions," he replied finally, "I'd trust him no more than a yard away, and then I'd want both his hands to be in sight. Here, I—well, I have to take him on faith. But," he added sternly, "don't *you* get in his way. He's nervous about more things than art."

"I won't," said I with fervor. "You said he was in this purely for revenge. What did Jay Ruber do to him?"

"Jay," said Barney with a rueful shake of his head, "did not behave in a nice way at all. Never mind that, though.—You see my problem. I can't interfere with those three before they start for the ransom meeting; for the sake of Melissa's safety, they have to be given as much rope as possible. I think we're still on the safe side; maybe they're doubtful, but I backed up my story as best I could when I made myself a new character as a bona fide tenant."

"I see. This whole masquerade was only to lend artistic verisimilitude—"

He took it up at once. "To an otherwise bald and unconvincing narrative; yes. I had to prepare for anything. What I was really dreading was a—uh, well, boyfriend of C. Ferris. It had to look as if you'd moved."

"Little did you know," I said, "what a small risk you ran from that quarter."

"I know now, but I didn't until I saw you." He sat down beside me. "How about friends from your office—where was it you said you worked?"

"Caya's. Wholesale hardware. I've been there only six weeks, but that's long enough; I don't ask my office acquaintances to come calling." (That was literally true, I hadn't asked Roger. But was it fair not to mention him—trying to put him out of my mind?)

"What do you do there?"

"I'm a filing clerk. I put away invoices about wire and bolts and shovels, so that nobody but me can find 'em again. Thus industry is carried on."

He chuckled. "What did you do before that?"

"Lived in Salem, Oregon, and nursed my father when he had arthritis, and helped bring up my sister's three little boys."

"All your life you've been doing that?"

"Oh, no. Before that I taught physical ed. in high school for a year, and before *that* I earned my board and keep at the University, the years when I wasn't working to get a little surplus. Good grief," I added, struck, "how drab and pathetic it sounds when it's described that way. Really, I had plenty of fun as I went along."

He was looking at me with interest. "You know," he said, "I begin to get it. That background, and the invoices, and having no close friends here—yes, that explains a lot."

"What?"

"Why you stood up to me instead of screaming, or giving in to that bluff; why you've taken everything in your stride since then. No, Cameron"—the name was deliberately used—"you haven't ruined things completely; but any other woman might have done it."

"Well, I'm glad," I said truthfully. "When I think about that baby, and how the parents must feel, I know why people want to lynch kidnappers."

He said slowly, "The child is our immediate problem, of course. That's the job I have to do, and I suppose the rest can be left to the newspaper men. But—oh, Lord, how I'd like to get in on that other part, too."

"You hate sitting here, don't you?"

"Yes, I hate it. There are amenities, of course." He flicked me with a glance. "I only hope I don't pay too much attention to those, in case I should be needed. But, damn it, I have to wait till I'm called on. I can't strike out on my own for fear of tipping over the balance. I want the kidnappers and I want to get them without endangering the baby's life."

"Barney—" I hesitated even to put it into words,—"after all this time, do you think she can be—still alive?"

"I hope so," he said tonelessly. "Jay and the others know it's to their advantage to keep her alive. Probably the woman's been taking some kind of care—"

His voice trailed off into silence. He leaned his head against the back of the chesterfield and shut his eyes.

I sat looking at him thoughtfully, realizing the strain under which he had been laboring. Perhaps I'd helped to ease it somewhat, by letting him talk; those terrible dragging hours of inaction had to be filled somehow. Let him rest now, I thought.

For all the fantastic aspects of our nearness in this cold dreary room, there was an oddly comfortable feeling between us. We might at this moment be a long-married couple who had sat up too late discussing our household budget.

—This won't *do*, Cameron, I told myself severely. A fine thing this is, sitting here playing house all by yourself, just because a man is beside you taking a little rest.—

In the quiet, I was taken unawares with a shattering yawn.

Barney sprang to attention at once. "If I'm not a heel!" he said remorsefully. "No mercy on the innocent bystander. Look, you're tired; I've talked your ear off. Why don't I go sit in the kitchen, so you can go to bed?"

"Bed!" I repeated incredulously. "Do you think I could sleep until this is over? That yawn didn't mean I was sleepy; it just meant—the room's chilly, and I had an early supper."

He fixed me with an interested gaze, and hopefully murmured, "Coffee?"

"Why not? Could you do with some—and have you time?"

He looked at the watch strapped to a massive wrist. "Ten after one. I have either an hour and a half or—all night. You know, there's a chance that the whole thing will be a washout and I won't be called at all."

I shook my head. "Don't ask me how I know it, but something's bound to happen. It's all around us—all through this building. Don't you feel that?"

"It may be wishful thinking; but if it's not, let's eat while the going is good. I'm afraid I used up some of the supplies." He gave me a comic glance of apology.

"You cad," I said with a grin, all at once feeling amazingly cheerful.

It was astonishing to find how useful he could be in a kitchen. The inappropriate fancy kept returning: Mama and Papa fixing a midnight snack before—no, skip that. Skip it very firmly. Agnes Cameron Ferris, you don't know this man. What if you do like his voice and the shape of his head? What if he can cap a silly quotation, or draw accurate conclusions about you from a few bald facts, or laugh at you so that you rather enjoy it? That isn't enough.—

You've got to have a good foundation: honor, and steadiness, and kindness. Don't forget.

The coffee was on the table, and Barney had been competently employing the toaster. He was now squatting before the low cupboard, rooting in its depths for a pot of jam. That was the moment he chose to ask, "Have you ever been in love?"

The question was elaborately casual; perversely, it made me think he really wanted to know. Coming on the heels of my own musings, too, it startled out of me the truth that no other human being had ever heard.

"Once," I said.

"What kind of a guy?" He didn't ask if I minded his questioning.

"A really nice guy," I said in a tone as offhand as his own. "He was a natural for a maiden's dream; tall and black haired and blue eyed, and charm oozing from every pore. It wasn't all on the surface, either; he's as regular as they come. He married my sister, so I know."

Raising his eyes to meet mine, Barney said, "H'm," far down in his throat.

"The trouble was I couldn't even resent it. Neither of them ever guessed how I felt, and—nobody on earth could be jealous of Merideth. She's lovely herself, all the way through."

"That her picture you had on your desk?"

"That's Merideth. She's closer to me than anyone on earth."

"She's beautiful, all right."

"It's more than that; there's a sort of champagne quality to her that had them swooning in droves."

"Those are her children—and his?"

I nodded.

"And you had to bring them up." There was comprehension in his level look.

"It wasn't so bad. I was through the worst by then. I knew from the beginning that I'd get over it someday."

"But it took a long time, I suppose."

I nodded again. Not until that moment had I known how complete was my recovery.

Barney said slowly, "And out of the hundreds of men who must have wanted to marry *you*—you never found a substitute?"

"Oh, not hundreds," I corrected him modestly. "They didn't quite reach three figures. Why, no—I never saw another one that suited. I knew too well what they wanted of me; a good housekeeper and mother, and a cheerful companion. Maybe I could have been those things, and felt tolerably happy; I was looking for someone who—who saw something more in me."

(And what on earth possessed me to come out with that? I'd never have said it to Roger Tripp, for fear of demanding something he couldn't give.)

"That's all?" Barney prompted.

"That's all. Short and simple annals."

"Hey," he said reproachfully after a brief silence, "you're missing a cue. I asked you—"

"Oh, I'm sorry. Wait till I get my voice right." It came out fine, throaty and languorous. "And—you?"

"Beautifully done." He grinned, and having finished his coffee, rose to get himself a drink of water. "I'll tell you; our slant on things is a bit different. I've thought I was in love, more than once; but it's never taken me to the point of marriage."

(Playing house without stopping to think that he might be married! That made it worse.)

"You see"—water from the faucet ran strongly into his glass, and he stood with his back to me, waiting for it to grow cold, letting it overflow—"you see, I'd always thought of women as something you took occasionally, like a highball—or champagne, if you like. It hadn't struck me till now that they might be a necessity, something you had to have daily. Like water," he finished thoughtfully, and removed the glass.

The stream from the faucet hit a spoon in the sink, and shot neatly upward right into his eye. I gave way to simple laughter.

Fortunately it struck him funny too. Between splutters, mopping his streaming face with a towel, he shook with suppressed chuckles. "I make no more figures of speech," he said, turning to face me. "Look here, what are you going to do after tonight—I mean, where do you plan to stay?"

"I expect I'd better get out of this palace of sin, a girl has to think of her reputation. The club might be the best bet; it's a parrot house, but it's beyond reproach."

"That sounds safe enough. Do they—uh—do they allow followers?"

"I believe so," I replied demurely. Both of us were still laughing. "There's a lovely parlor for entertaining callers. It has an overhead light and some very hard sofas, and in the center is a table, and on the table is something that I *think* is an aspidistra."

"No!" said Barney, awed.

"I don't guarantee that, I'm no botanist."

"It's a long time since I've seen an aspidistra," he remarked wistfully. "If I put on my best clothes, and came to call tomorrow night—or the next night, when you've had some rest—"

"You'd have to bring references," I said as his voice trailed off, and then glanced up at him.

All the merriment had left his face, and he spoke in a low tone. "I was forgetting—what has to be done tonight."

"But why can't you—Barney, do you mean that the danger you talked about—"

"Oh, yes. It's there, sure enough. Even without the unknown factor, Fingers and Jay have to be dealt with. They're impetuous, I hear.—Don't look like that," he added in a curiously shaken tone.

I don't know how I'd been looking, but my eyes dropped.

Barney waited a minute before he spoke again. "Colly O'Shea is on my side, and until now I hadn't worried about the risk. What I do regret is having brought you into this mess."

In as neutral a voice as I could manage, I said, "I don't mind."

He knew too much about me already to be deceived by that. "Understatement of the week," he remarked derisively. "You're having the time of your life. Well, Cameron, you listen to me. As far as you're concerned, the excitement is all over. As soon as I leave this place, you lock the window and put a chair under the doorknob, and don't so much as stick your nose outside, no matter what happens."

"But—while you're here?" I murmured with spurious meekness.

"I will protect you, cried Dick Dauntless, flexing his muscles," Barney replied; but there was a false note in that, too, and I looked at him once more.

He was consulting his watch; he frowned, and looked down the hall. I felt guilty, as if I'd been luring him from his duty with this irrelevant chat. "Shut away up here," he said, "I could wait all night and never know what went on. Supposing the whole thing's called off—or supposing it's shifted to another scene, or something's gone wrong. Could Garwood let me know in time?"

"I thought your job was to sit here," said I crisply.

Barney gave a short laugh. "If I said that, I was fooling myself. I'd no more miss the chance of getting my hands on those people! There's got to be some way that I—and Colly O'Shea—" He was thinking aloud now. "Colly's too anxious for his share."

"What do you think he might do?"

"Gum the works somehow. If he gets hold of Jay or Fingers before they can leave, his instincts might be too much for him. He doesn't give a damn for the baby. All he wants—"

I suggested, "Why don't you go next door and put the fear of the Lord into him?"

Barney said, "The Lord Himself would have a hard time doing that. But—maybe I'd better talk to him again." In his sudden restlessness, I thought, any action would be welcome. He was down the hall before he had finished speaking. I followed on his heels.

"Here," he added sharply, turning on me, "you're not going."

"Why not?" I demanded. "I'm as eager as you for something to happen. I know the story now, I might as well see as much as possible while you're here."

He hesitated, and then gave in grudgingly. "I suppose it can't do any harm. Just as well to have you under my eye as long as—No, no! Not through the hall. He'd never answer the bell. We'll have to use the window."

He had darkened the living room when we moved into the kitchen. Now all the lights were out, even in the public corridor; no line of brightness showed under my door. It was the thrifty habit of the household to plunge the halls into darkness at one o'clock each night.

I could see Barney only as a vague shadowy bulk drifting across the living room. He raised the shade, and the sky outside, faintly lit by the reflection of city lights on the low hanging clouds, showed barely two degrees brighter than the darkness of the room.

The window went up almost without a sound. "Oiled," he breathed in answer to my cautiously whispered question. A gust of wet wind swept in on us, fluttering the curtains, and Barney breathed of it deeply as he leaned out to scan the fire escape and the alley below.

"Blacker than the Earl of Hell's riding boots," I heard him mutter. "I'll get out first; don't come yet. You last, my dear Gaston—"

He was out on the iron platform, moving quietly toward the projecting bay window of the next apartment. I could see it dimly, the section nearest me unshaded as it must have been earlier when the three had slipped out. Keeping close against the wall, Barney scratched gently on the wood of the window frame.

He waited, and scratched again. The window was open a crack at the bottom; quietly he pushed it up and slid inside.

After a wait which was probably not long enough for prudence, I followed him. With eyes growing accustomed to the dark, I could see the faintly outlined shapes of furniture, and the blacker rectangles of open doors. This apartment was much larger than mine. From barely perceptible sounds I gathered that Barney was searching the other rooms.

He came back alone.

"What's hap—" I began, and was cut off by a venomous whisper.

"Gone, damn his hide! Gone off somewhere, maybe poking his nose into things and ruining the whole set-up. If I could get my hands on Colly I'd take him apart, so help me."

"He didn't just walk out on you?"

"Not unless he's crossed me up. And—somehow, you know, I don't believe he'd do that."

His tone sent another small shiver across my skin.

"Look, Barney; he couldn't possibly have gone to sleep, waiting?" I turned to the chesterfield, leaning over to feel the cushions.

"I looked there," said the faint whisper. "D'you think he slipped down the crack? Not but what I've found some—What is it?"

Crouching, feeling under the sofa, for one dreadful moment I couldn't speak; my fingers had touched leather, a heel, a lace, and I was afraid that Colly O'Shea had been found.

But beyond what I had touched was emptiness, and with a breath of relief I said, "His shoes; they're here on the floor."

I was startled by the headlong, silent rush across the room, and the appalled breathiness of Barney's voice in my ear. "His shoes!" The words hissed in the darkness as he knelt immobile, his back to the windows.

They were within my direct line of vision, the three parts of the bay window. The southern one, through which we had entered, was open, the other two were closed but unshaded. Through the left-hand one I could see to the north, up the alley, along the fire platform which ran the length of the house's rear wall.

At the far end of the building something moved, no more distinguishable than black on black, except for that slow stirring.

"Look, out there!" I breathed, "I saw something—" and was at the window, straining my eyes, before Barney's peremptory whisper reached me.

"Cameron! Get away from there!" He came beside me, jerked at my shoulder. "Get *down*—"

I remember twisting half around, and the shadow outside looming suddenly large in the corner of my eye.

Then the sky fell on me.

SEVEN

Later Than You Think

POSSIBLY I WAS unconscious for a minute, not more than that. Afterward I could hear, and feel, and even get my eyes open to see that the roof and the windows were whole. It couldn't, I conjectured dimly, have been a bomb; yet something had all but jarred my bones loose from their moorings.

What I heard was more whispering. "You fool, you incredible fool!" it said hopelessly. Was that addressed to me?

What I felt was a pair of hands, gentle and impersonal as a surgeon's, passing over my body.

Lying still, dizzily I took stock. It was all right, wasn't it? Those massive shoulders looming above me must be Barney's. I was not actually hurt, evidently I'd fallen relaxed. There was just one minor annoyance: I couldn't breathe.

And why did the whisper now seem to come from the far corner of the room? No, there must be two people here, for the one above me said simply, "Shut up."

This whisper died away, and Barney's fingers rested over my heart. I gave a feeble flop and tried once more to draw breath. "Coming out of it," sounded from overhead.

I tried to corroborate him on that point, but all that emerged was a wheeze like the last strains of a parlor organ.

The voice across the room now became more audible, and revealed its owner as Mr. O'Shea. But where had he come from?

"I think," he said contemptuously, "that her wind is knocked out."

I wished that brick wall could have fallen on *him*. "Yeah," I managed to produce from the top of one lung, and Barney's hand went away like a rocketing pheasant.

He seemed relieved, though. "You sure? Then just lie still for a few minutes." I was lifted, seemed to float across the room, and found myself on the chesterfield. The shadow that had carried me turned away.

Oxygen, in ever increasing quantities, helped a good deal. The ringing sensation left my head. I lay and breathed gratefully, and tried without shame to hear what the two men were saying, since they were not quite out of earshot. A quarrel conducted in whispers and pitch darkness is a very odd thing to listen to.

Barney said, "—what I have to do, trying to cover up—"

Mutter, mutter, from O'Shea.

"Tonight of all nights! You should have—"

More muttering.

Barney's voice was lowered; he was telling off O'Shea about something, for the answering murmur was unmistakably sullen.

Then the deep voice said, quite audibly, "You hear me? Back they go."

"Have it your way." Mr. O'Shea seemed to be capitulating, but against his will.

And then, after a long indistinguishable colloquy, the word "ice" emerged aloud, at the end of a sentence.

Obsessed with my own solar plexus, I construed this as a new treatment. "No," I croaked imploringly, "no ice—on me. Too cold. I'm—getting better—"

They broke off, suddenly aware that the word had been audible; and then, for some reason, gave way to amusement. A subdued chuckle came from Barney, and a kind of snort from O'Shea. Barney left him, and came to bend over me.

"Cameron," he said, "I'm sorry—sorrier than I can express. That knockout was my fault, clumsy ass that I am. I was only trying to—to protect you, pull you out of sight, but we tripped each other somehow and went down together in a heap."

"Nice—you meant—well. What—what was—"

"It was only Colly," he reassured me. "I—I didn't know that, of course. I was afraid that Jay or Fingers—you can see how it was, I couldn't stop to make sure. You were in full sight at that window."

"Colly?—Where—from?"

Barney waited a second too long before answering. Then he said, "He came up the fire ladder. He'd been down below, looking around."

I lay silent, struggling to bring back memory. Surely that dark form I had seen was at the end of the platform, far beyond the ladder? And wasn't it bent double, as if climbing in or out of somewhere? But if I believed that mental picture correct—it would mean that someone was lying.

The certainty filled my mind. Barney was holding something back.

But wasn't I on his side, and didn't I feel safe while I was with him? I'd ignore that contradictory picture, push it firmly away from me.

"Well, thanks," I gasped. "But—something like—sack of cement in my stomach—"

"That was my head," said Barney with some asperity, and I gave a painful moan which had started as a laugh. "You're sure you're not hurt anywhere else?"

"No. No, I'll be all right."

"I thought I'd killed you. The fact that you weren't—actually in danger made it worse."

Now I could draw breath enough for a sentence. "I guess you just don't know your own strength."

"It isn't my practice," he said with humility, "to butt ladies in the middle."

"I suppose not." I was able to sit up at last. "But if you don't mind, next time just touch me on the shoulder. I'll fall flat on my face at once, I promise you."

"The occasion," said Barney, "will not arise. You're going back into your apartment. I was an idiot to let you come in here."

"At least," I said, painfully scrambling to my feet, "you're even with me now for laughing about the water in your face. Like as not you arranged this on purpose."

Mr. O'Shea, almost forgotten in the gloom behind us, giggled again. He spoke with an unpleasant softness. "If he does nothing worse than that—"

"Colly." Barney's voice cut across the sentence, deliberate, cold with a paralyzing lack of expression. "That—will—be—plenty."

I found myself frantically hoping that that tone would never be used on me.

O'Shea made no answer but a step forward. The very ease of his movement had the indefinable quality of anger. He was ready once more to mutiny; but something held him in check.

It was a domination invisibly, silently expressed, that came from the still figure beside me like a shock from electrified wire. The other man began to speak again, and stopped on the first word. Slowly, slowly, the flame of anger was beaten down. I knew almost the exact moment when it died.

"I've done my best for you, haven't I?" said Barney quietly. The level voice took victory for granted. "You don't see it that way now, but later you will."

"Perhaps you are right." The thin man was regaining his suavity.

"No reprisals, then. You'll keep your promise, as I'm keeping mine."

"I will keep it. For tonight only, you are calling the moves."

"Okay. I'll see you later," said Barney, and with a light touch on my arm urged me toward the window.

I wasn't going to think any more, nor try to figure out any of the inexplicable things I'd heard. Somehow, Barney must have acted for the best; believe that, forget everything else. Presumably he'd achieved the purpose of his visit, to check up on a doubtful ally.

I crawled shakily out to the fire escape, and stood once more in my own apartment. Barney stayed by the window for a moment, and seemed to be listening. No sound came to my ears, but he appeared satisfied, for the window went down.

I groped for the lamp and turned it on, blinking in the flood of light. His eyes went over me from head to foot. "Honestly, you're not hurt?" he repeated.

"Oh, of course not. Didn't I tell you it was all right? Just wash it out."

He gave me a brief grin. "You'll do to take along, Cameron. I guess you could always be counted on, to be a good sport."

Next to "wholesome," "a good sport" is the most damning summary of a woman that you can make. Probably I hadn't yet got over the technical knockout, for physical shock and a lifelong irritation combined to loosen my tongue. "Yes," I said, turning on him with involuntary violence, "I've spent years earning that reputation, in default of anything better. Good old Ronnie—good pal—good sport!"

His brows drew together. "Pitch into me if you like," he said mildly. "You have every right. But keep it quiet."

The irritation faded, and left me feeling ashamed. "I don't want to pitch into you. Sorry it sounded that way. And I know I oughtn't to shout, and—turn lights on. You meant this room to be dark, didn't you?"

Barney stood with his hands in his pockets, looking at me with an unreadable expression. "It would be better, as a matter of fact; but I thought—"

"I don't want to spoil anything more." The dark, I reflected as I snapped the light button, might be soothing to jangled nerves.—Sit down, Cameron, and compose yourself. Complaining, at a time like this! As if you hadn't said enough already, out in the kitchen!

But this darkness had the wrong effect. Something in the room felt different; I was uneasy and couldn't define the reason. Once my pupils were expanded, I could make out the dim shapes of furniture. Barney had moved to the far side of the room. He was sitting in the hard armchair, quite silent.

"You're still—waiting for something to happen?" Even my subdued murmur was startlingly loud in the black quiet.

"Still waiting," he said after a pause.

"It couldn't have come off while we were in the next room? What time is it?"

"Not two yet." He was silent once more.

Did he think he could get away with this? After that cock-eyed melodrama next door, just to sit down quietly and say nothing was like being dropped twenty feet. If he'd only talk!

"You're asking too much," I burst out suddenly in a stage whisper. "I can't take *everything* in my stride."

"What's bothering you now?" Barney asked remotely.

"Plenty. O'Shea, for one thing. It's because I don't know anything about him that he's frightening. Can't you see that, Barney? You tell me half a story and then stop dead and expect me to be satisfied. Why can't I be told what lies behind this affair? There's something more, of course."

He stirred in the darkness. "So you've guessed that."

"How could I help it? You called the enemy 'unknown,' but you talked as if you knew him—knew more than you've told me, anyway."

"Maybe I do," said Barney, "and maybe not. There's a chance that he doesn't exist at all, that somebody just dreamed him up, and Jay and Fingers used his name for the kidnapping to throw Cleveland off the scent; but somehow he seems real to me."

It was just as I'd thought. The minute he started to talk, the tension slackened. I wanted to hear the story, but more than that I wanted to feel comfortable again, to regain that feeling of easy comradeship into which we had slipped by such imperceptible degrees.

"Go on," I said. "What about that chain of circumstances that forced his hand?"

"Yes, I'll go on," Barney said, getting to his feet. "I've hinted too much already, haven't I? You might as well hear about the other thing. In a way, it's bigger and more serious even than the kidnapping."

"More serious?"

He began to wander slowly up and down the length of the room. I could barely see where he was. From different points in the dark his low murmur reached me like spirit voices at a séance.

"Maybe kidnapping is the worst crime you can think of. Everyone hates it, everyone feels for the child and the parents, but personally it doesn't affect more than a very few. And the thing behind this doesn't sound like much. No one but the staff of the *Eagle* has got very excited about it. It's in the background, but—look at it this way: the crime against the Clevelands is like a play that wouldn't have been put on at all without that backdrop. That's a feeble metaphor, but I can't think of a better. It stems from another crime, and that from—from something that doesn't look like a crime at all.

"I didn't tell you this earlier, because it's the darnedest story you ever heard. You've been believing what I told you, haven't you? Yes, because it hangs together; you can see me, you know the baby was here, you read the news item about Mrs. Ulrichson.

"But I'm afraid you won't believe this."

I said, "You know what the White Queen used to do before breakfast?"

"Believe seven impossible things, wasn't it?" He chuckled faintly.

"Six. I think that after she'd got past the first one, the other five were comparatively easy."

"Okay, Queen, I'll try you out," said Barney. A match flared, stamping his face in yellow light on black shadow. He lit his cigarette, and gave me one while the flame lasted. Then the glowing coal, waxing and waning, suspended six feet in the air, wandered about the room as if the spirits had gone into Technicolor as well as sound. Occasionally when he drew on it I could see his face, but you can't gauge a person's expression from so brief a glimpse.

He said, "Let's begin with a spot of catechism. What makes the biggest news these days?"

"The war."

"Right. And—in America?"

"That's not so obvious. Defense, maybe? Aid to Britain?"

"Right again. What newspaper do you read?"

"Either of the big morning dailies, when I happen to buy one. That does not send you twenty-five dollars and a set of the Britannica."

"That's too bad," said Barney. "I mean, that you don't read the *Eagle*. This would be easier if you knew something about the Cork."

"But this way," I pointed out maliciously, "you get a chance to tell me all about it."

"Look here," he said hotly, "if you think I'm in the habit of talking for hours on end—who asked for an explanation, anyhow?" I drew on my cigarette. He broke off, laughing. "Oh, Lord—ribbed by an expert. Just for that I'll tell you at length. Doesn't the word Cork convey anything to your mind?"

"Life belts," I said obligingly. "Ferdinand the Bull. Cigarette tips."

"You're miles off."

"Wine bottles—"

"Getting warmer. If you'd said bottlenecks, now, you'd have been right in there.

"You know how newspapers are. They hold out for picturesque speech at all costs, and that title was one of their little inventions. The *Eagle*'s public likes that sort of thing. They've been following the stories on the Cork as if he were Superman."

"Well, who is he? A sort of mythical hero?"

"No," said Barney, "I wouldn't call him that." He paused for a long moment. Then he went on:

"About three months ago, the *Eagle* got a hot lead. Being a labor paper, it had inside channels of information. The story was exclusive, too, because nobody else would touch it. It was too fantastic."

"Don't tell me," I said, "I know what comes next. They found a wild-eyed man with a strong German accent and a bomb in his hand, creeping around the training camps."

"I wish they had. It would have been something definite, and the F.B.I. would have done the investigation. As it was—there wasn't anything you could put your finger on, only a crazy yarn that a reporter brought in."

❀❀❀

...The reporter's name was Mangam. He'd been given a running assignment on Labor in defense; and, since he was passionately convinced of the essential patriotism of Labor, he required lots of proof before he'd believe any rumors of sabotage.

Strikes, he thought, did not come under this heading. They were openly conducted, and in a time of big contracts and rising prices they were all but inevitable. It was a theory of his that a gradual slowing of production was more serious in the long run than a stoppage of work which could be arbitrated. With the rest of the country, however, he realized that production was not up to schedule.

There were a few isolated cases that bothered him, cases where a time lag could be traced directly to one dissatisfied or incompetent person. Workers in big industries sometimes talk bitterly of being only cogs in a machine. A faulty cog can be easily replaced, but the replacement causes delay.

Mangam began a survey, tracing as many of these cases as could be reached. What was causing them, accident or design? If the latter, were the workers aware of it? He was ever their friend, and he couldn't help fearing that they might be persuaded or fooled into dangerous indifference.

Up to the end of the year he'd made little progress; the individuals proved elusive, and, when run to ground, vague in their statements. Then the Government began to let contracts for the new shipyards across the Bay, and Mangam was in at the start of a project. He had no concern with the slow untangling of government red tape. He went straight for what he knew, the human element; and he began to find some indications that puzzled him.

There was, for instance, the truck driver who had such bad luck with tires; they seemed to attract long spikes. His engine gave lots of trouble, too, and twice during the winter rains his truck bogged down on a soft shoulder of the highway. Each time the load that he carried was vitally needed; each time there was a delay of several hours.

There was the mistake in copying blueprints, which was discovered almost at once; but before a new set of prints could be made, the yard construction was delayed three days.

There was the case of a stenographer, discharged for small inaccuracies in transmitting orders. In her former job, she had been thoroughly trustworthy. She was reticent about her work in the shipyard office, but finally let it be known that her seeming inaccuracy had been the fault of careless dictation, and the blame had been meanly placed on her. That was her story, but her mistakes had caused irritating delays—and she had a new fur coat.

(At this point I sat up, my skin suddenly prickling.)

One small instance followed another, and in every one the same word cropped up with what seemed to Mangam an ominous persistence. *Delay*: delay of a few hours, delay of two days or a week—he added them up once, allowing for overlaps, and the total frightened him. He knew all too well that in these days a war might be lost because help came a few months too late. That five-letter word became almost an obsession with him, as it was with the heads of the Defense Commission; but he felt that in his small investigation he was dealing with something as fundamentally important as their problems of production. Little by little he became convinced that there was a single cause for the delays on the shipyard project; the cases were oddly similar in their innocent appearance and their insidious danger…

"Wait," I said. "Wait just a minute. That's the new shipyard in Oakland, the one that's building cargo vessels for Britain?"

"Yes."

"You don't by any chance know who the contractor is?"

"A man named Flaherty, I think."

"Holy Moses in the bulrushes!"

"What is it? Do you know Flaherty?"

"I think—I believe it was that stenographer who got me in trouble!" I had the thrill that comes with the sudden solution of a mystery. "No wonder they said it was so important. No wonder the Smith man got excited! Why of course, I can see it now. She could destroy the original order—spill ink on it or something—and type another, with that error that seemed so natural; but it was done on purpose!"

I was jabbering elliptically, as if Barney knew all about it. The thing had finally to be explained, and he came and stood beside me, listening with close attention.

Somehow Roger's part in the episode was minimized. It was mean of me, but I told myself that it was beside the point.

"I see," Barney said when I'd finished. "It's touched you too—only that one little manifestation, but you can see how it works. The mistake was cleared up, you say? How much time was lost?"

"Over a week."

"Uh-huh. There it is. Once or twice it could happen; but when there are so many cases—and it's not as if the shipyards were the only instance, there have been dozens of others. Well, Mangam got his cockeyed story."

...Someone talked. He wouldn't say who, nor was that important, but the story was that these delays were fabricated, not by the persons immediately responsible, but by another person who hired them. The risks were small. The worker seldom lost his job; criminal intent could not be proved, nobody was hurt or endangered by his act; he was a hundred dollars or so to the good—and above all, he would be most unlikely to disclose that he had been bribed into this brief disloyalty, whose consequences might be so far reaching.

Mangam's friend, however, did talk. The person who paid him, he said, had never identified himself. Mangam's friend had seen him—oh, yes, more than once; a big man with a stubby mustache, prominent ears, deep-set eyes. You'd think it would be easy to find him again, but he appeared only to carry on his negotiations, which began cautiously by telephone and ended with one personal interview and the pay-off. Those who had met this gentleman on business rather esteemed his generous habits, but they couldn't pursue a social life in his company because no one knew his name or where he lived...

"From that description he might be anybody," Barney said, striking one hand into the other, "anybody who doesn't have to explain his absences. It's a man, that's all we know, probably tall. For his size, there's such a thing as padding."

"And false whiskers," I murmured.

"Yes." He was quite serious. "The ears could be made to stand out from his head with a bit of putty—no one has ever got close enough to take a good look; and thick eyebrows, pasted on, could give the impression—"

"Come," I said, "you're forgetting the red suit with white fur trimming."

He gave a short unwilling chuckle. "I said you wouldn't believe me. Wait, though; see if you think this is funny."

...The *Eagle* had received Mangam's story with interest not untempered by amusement. It was a good yarn, if it hadn't possessed such a strong flavor of movie serial; here was the favorite ingredient, the Mystery Man, arriving out of the nowhere and disappearing into the same when his villainy had been accomplished. They gave it a trial spin in the next day's paper, with the humorous angle to the fore. If anything came of it, the serious aspects could be played up later.

Mangam refused to laugh. He kept on with his ferreting, and the *Eagle* staff, scrutinizing the results, began to think that they had something. They made up a name for the big man with the mustache. He was the Cork, who stopped up a bottleneck.

They were even more encouraged when, under this fire of publicity, the artificial delays became less frequent. The story, however, was too good to drop. It was "stock news, *must*."

Then, to their great delight, they received a threat, a facsimile of which was promptly reproduced in the paper. Mailed in San Francisco, on cheap paper absolutely virgin of fingerprints, printed from a purple ink-pad with rubber-stamp letters, it read, "Lay off the Cork, or else."

That, everyone felt, might be a joke of sorts. The other newspapers, in fact, believed that Mangam had sent it himself to bolster up his story. On the other hand, it might mean that the reporter was close on the trail. That was his own contention, the only trouble being that he didn't recognize the lead that he'd accidentally struck. What was more, his quest was leading him into some very queer company; but he went on...

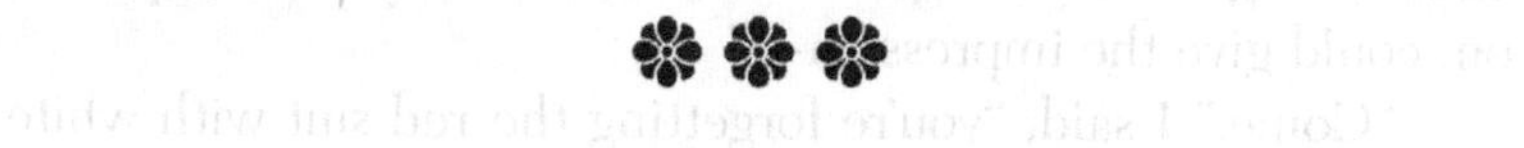

"They can't intimidate an editor?" I suggested.

Barney laughed without mirth. "It wasn't quite like that. Mangam wouldn't have dropped it for anything you could offer. There was just one way to stop him."

"Oh, he did stop?"

"He was killed," said Barney tonelessly.

EIGHT

Reasonable Facsimile

THERE HAD BEEN some excitement about that in the papers. A saloon brawl had spilled out onto a dark street in the East Bay, and Mangam was found in an alley, unconscious and with a fractured skull. He died a week later.

His money was gone, and so was the mini-camera which he had been carrying. The unused rolls of film in his pockets had been examined and left behind. Almost at once someone was arrested for the crime—a character of notoriously rough habits, who, as the police appeared, was trying to get rid of Mangam's wallet.

Wildly this captive protested his innocence. It was a couple of other fellows, he hadn't been near Mangam till he found him unconscious, and then—who could be blamed for picking up a bit of loose change? The real murderer, he added, must have been the big man whom Mangam had been eyeing in the saloon. Yes, that was it; the description grew more detailed; it was a man with eyes that sank far back into his head, and conspicuous ears. It was, in fact, the Cork.

The rough character was laughed to scorn. Was he sure, the police asked merrily, that the Blue Fairy hadn't appeared round a corner and bashed Mangam with the brick which had been found near him? That story would be as likely. There was no such person as the Cork.

The rough character was firmly placed in the clink, and nobody—not even the few who believed his story—felt that this was a miscarriage of justice.

Those who believed him, however, were the members of the *Eagle* staff. Now, of all times, they could not give up.

Another reporter, Garwood, was assigned to the story. He couldn't pick up the lead on which Mangam had unconsciously stumbled, but he went at it from the other end.

At this point the story began to get complicated. One careless word, one slip in timing would have changed the whole pattern, and Melissa Cleveland would never have been in danger. On the other hand, the death of Mangam might have gone forever unavenged. Luck worked with a nice impartiality.

The staff of the *Eagle* had built up a mental picture: the blow, the snatching of the camera, the examination of the remaining film packs to make sure that the one bearing important evidence was not among them—the quick departure. They took for granted that the camera was either destroyed or in the possession of the Cork. Garwood, however, knew the registration number. With only a faint hope of success, he set out to trace it with the help of the East Bay police.

They circulated the number to various pawnshops and camera dealers. Early on Monday, the eighth, a pawnbroker virtuously telephoned the Oakland headquarters, to say that he had the camera; of course, he'd had *no* idea that it was stolen goods.

As bad luck would have it, a reporter from one of the other papers was at the station when the call came in. Mangam's death was still news, he saw no reason to suppress the discovery, and on

Monday night the item appeared—without, however, a description of the person who had done the pawning. Garwood and the police were given that on Monday morning. They had the whole day to work in, but someone else was close on their heels.

The Cork did not have the camera, never had had it. It had passed out of Mangam's possession before either he or his pursuer had stepped into the dark street where he met his death; it had either been left in the saloon or stolen from him there. The film pack, for which the Cork had committed his futile murder, was still at large—somewhere unknown, for it had been missing when the camera was pawned.

Acting with speed and justifiable caution, Garwood found the saloon waiter who had "picked up" the camera; and with diplomacy, a promise of immunity and a bit of lagniappe, got from him the information that marked a turning point. With some crude idea of eluding detection, the waiter had removed the film; and by an incredibly lucky chance he had kept it.

Nobody knew whether the Cork somehow found this out, or whether he merely jumped to the correct conclusion. The important thing was that he learned it, though Garwood had several hours' start on him. Early on Tuesday morning, the waiter received a telephone call, purporting to be from Garwood himself.

Probably he never realized how near he was to death when he answered that call.

"Garwood speaking. That film you were to deliver—I've changed my mind about it. I'll come for it myself, this morning."

The waiter was sullen and yawning after a night of work. "Don't bother, buddy," he snapped back. "You're too late. I didn't want to handle it after what you told me—phoned the old woman last night, and told her to stick it in the mailbox."

A pause. "It's already in the mail?"

"You heard me, chum. Whatsa matter, you afraid the police'll get it after all? Not a chance."

"Are you sure you sent it to the right place? Repeat that address for me."

For a minute everything hung balanced; then weariness and bad temper pressed down the scale on the side of justice—and its slow descent took a small child into deadly peril.

"Ah, the hell with it. Sure I got the address right. You'll get it as soon as if I'd took it there myself," the waiter said, and slammed down the receiver.

The hanging evidence was in the mail. There was no telling where it would go; but the two most likely places were the *Eagle* office and Garwood's home in the city. If it had been picked up in the morning, it could not be delivered before eleven at the earliest; the afternoon delivery was more probable. The Cork had two hours or more in which to work. It was a short period, but it would serve.

He could not have anticipated this very set of circumstances, but for a long time he must have known that someday the unrelenting pursuit would catch up with him. Without doubt he had planned far ahead, held his forces in readiness. Perhaps he had recruited them on the day when Mangam first guessed at his existence. If the camera had not been found, if the *Eagle* had accepted the fortuitous scapegoat who was now in jail for Mangam's murder, the move could have been postponed. Now, although it put him into further danger, he must strike. He must be able to make the one threat which would force the *Eagle*'s editor into submission.

He acted himself, or he gave the word to his employees. Jay and Gertie promptly obeyed.

There were two more mysterious telephone calls, one to the *Eagle*, one to Garwood's wife. "This is the Cork. When that film comes, leave it alone. You'll know why soon enough."

The calls were made at 10:30 on Tuesday morning—when the baby was already in the hands of her captors. At the moment, their recipients listened dazed and uncomprehending, but soon enough they knew why, indeed. Perhaps they would have obeyed this order, if it had been within their power.

Garwood had ordered the film sent to an East Bay camera shop. It had arrived at ten o'clock, and before the news of the kidnapping had reached him, before he could countermand his instructions, it had been developed…

❀ ❀ ❀

"They have a photograph of the Cork?" I demanded breathlessly.

"No," Barney said. "Here's the most hideous irony of the whole thing; it was all useless, all of it—the death, the threats, the danger. Mangam had failed. Only one shot in that whole film pack was any good. That was of a man with his arm over his face. It can't possibly be identified."

"But—the Cork doesn't know that?"

"That's what they believe—Cleveland and the staff of the *Eagle*. The secret has been kept like grim death; I suppose I'm the only outsider who knows it. The ransom payment must look as if it's on the up and up."

"But, good heavens," I said, "the Cork seems to know everything else. How can they be sure he hasn't found out about that too?"

"They can't be. They can only hope that he'll keep the baby alive until he's collected the ransom, and give us a chance to save her. They hope, because he's got a big stake in this, and he's been pushed farther than he'd meant to go.

"You see how he's been forced by circumstance? Up to the middle of January, he'd kept absolutely within the law. I don't believe, myself, that he meant to kill Mangam. Maybe the blow was harder than he'd meant it to be. Until that minute, the evidence he supposed was on the film wouldn't even have got him a jail sentence, it would only have finished his racket. Now—he's got a murder rap coming.

"He'd calculate the risk. The evidence, important as it might be, would seem to the editor a small price to pay for the safe return of his baby. It was double or nothing; maybe, if the Cork could hire someone to do the actual kidnapping, the odds would be in his favor. Steal a stack of chips, bet them all—and then if he won, return the stolen chips and call it a day. After that he could lie low for a while, and when he felt safe, start up in business somewhere else—out of the *Eagle*'s territory.

"What could be neater? He stole the chips from the very man he was trying to out-bet! And yet, though he takes big chances, I think he won't do anything he doesn't have to do."

"But what if—he found out that the evidence was worthless?"

Barney stood quite still for a moment. Then he said, "You can't hang twice."

"That's so," I whispered.

He took another turn around the room. "You see?" His voice drifted back from somewhere near the door. "A nice mess, isn't it?"

"I never heard anything like it in my life," I said. "It's—it's—has nobody an idea who the Cork is?"

"They've figured out this much; when he appears and disappears it's out of another life altogether—obviously one where nobody could suspect him, where his looks and manner are entirely different. People on these obscure secret jobs are chosen because they look ordinary or unlikely. For all we know, the Cork might be a Nob Hill socialite, or one of the salesmen in your office. He might be your neighbor Fingers Lossert-Spelvin. He might," Barney added with a ring of doubt his voice, "be Colly O'Shea."

Or you, I thought: and to my horror, heard myself saying it aloud!

"Or me," he agreed, unmoved. "I'm sure of my own innocence, but nobody else can be—except the Cork himself. I guess Walter Cleveland hasn't suspected me seriously."

I hadn't myself. That habit of thinking aloud would get me in trouble sometime.

"But isn't it more than likely," I said, "that he's one of the three kidnappers?"

"Maybe. If we catch them, we'll try to find out."

A very definite prickle went up my spine.

"Maybe!" he repeated bitterly. "Supposing what I said was true, and he doesn't exist, and the *Eagle* was just playing games. Those three crooks could have turned the story to their own ends and framed the little man who wasn't there. That'd be Frankenstein's monster for you. Oh, hell—I've thought it over until I'm cockeyed. And yet—all the signs point to it, to one person who's a genius at organization, who can think fast enough to deal with any situation, who knows just the right attitude to take with everyone he works with.

"And that double-or-nothing prospect—he wouldn't have taken such a risk if he didn't have a getaway planned; he'll either get caught or he'll be completely safe and above suspicion, back in that other life that looks so innocent— Why, look; suppose it were Bassett, here."

"Bassett?"

"The landlady's nephew; your quavering friend."

"From my one look at Mr. Bassett," I said, "I think he prefers his bottles wide open at the neck."

"It's not likely, I'll admit. When we found out about Mrs. Ulrichson's accident, the reporters were curious enough to check up on Bassett. He's exactly what he makes out to be; lives alone in a cottage over in the East Bay somewhere, and runs a little two-for-a-nickel grocery that barely makes him a living. He has some of the neighbors in to play pinochle, every now and then. He takes pictures of their kids with a Brownie, he digs in his garden.—Garwood asked the boy who works in the store if it wasn't hard for Mr. Bassett to get away. The boy was pleased as Punch to be left in charge. He says, 'Mr. Bassett lets me keep store lots of times when he's visiting his Auntie in Frisco.' Well—"

"Well?"

"Bassett's improbable, but no more so than anyone else. He's alibied for all the important times, though I suppose he could have hired these thugs to do all the dirty work. —Oh, what's the use? I get something like that all figured out, and then I call myself a fool for suspecting him, or anyone. That's not my job."

All at once his voice deflated, as if exhaustion had overtaken him. He added, "There's your story. Will that hold you?" and sat down at last, but still on the hard chair across the room.

"You know how women are," I said. "Give 'em an inch and they grab for the yardstick. How much more time do we have?"

"Lord knows."

"Then clear up everything for me. Tell me what actually happened when you knocked me out next door."

He was silent momentarily; then he spoke with an unusual stiffness in his tone. "I've been doing my best to forget that affair next door. I'm not proud of it. Do we have to bring it up again?"

"No, no, you've got it all wrong. I'm not holding a grudge, you know that. I only wondered—"

"Stop," said Barney levelly. "Stop right there."

Considerably daunted, I did stop. He said nothing more. There we sat, once more strangers and enemies, with a thick wall of darkness and silence between us.

What was it that had gone wrong? He must know by now that I didn't mean to reproach him; but if that were the case, there was no reason for his suddenly getting angry.

I honestly could not think what the trouble was.

He shifted uncomfortably in the small chair, and it creaked under his weight. I said in a small voice of apology, "I think that chair petrified in the store basement. Why don't you come back to the chesterfield?"

"Safer to stay here," said the disembodied voice.

"What on earth are you—" I began, and then a horrible and mortifying conviction got me by the throat.

I'd said too much. He was answering, deliberately, as if explaining in words of one syllable.

"I promised I'd be a perfect gent, didn't I? Well, I'm not. When I was touching you, there in the next room, to find out if you were hurt—I might have found the pulse in your wrist. But I didn't, as you damn well know. And now—I want to touch you again."

For an instant I remembered, too, and my whole body started awake as if his hand once more rested over my heart. It was sickening to feel it, against will and logic and decency—because I knew that he'd had to say that, and I knew the reason.

"That's not why I asked you to come back here." My voice was dreary and toneless, and I caught back an unsteady breath.

In a second he was on his feet. "Cameron," he said. "Cameron—you're not crying?" With noiseless swiftness he crossed the room. His shoulders bulked large, close to me; he was kneeling by the arm of the chesterfield so that my head was nearly as high as his. I saw in his hand a faint glimmer of something white, and realized that he was kindly preparing to dry my tears.

At the sight, absurdly enough, I very nearly did cry.

"Go away," I said in a strangled whisper. "I don't need a handkerchief."

"I didn't mean to frighten you. Lord knows," Barney said, "I meant to keep quiet. You needn't tell me this is no time for love-making, but—"

"Don't," I said. "Please don't." On this feeble plea my breath gave out entirely.

"No," he said, misunderstanding—and deliberately stretched out a hand on either side of me, "—I won't touch you again; but I want to know what's the matter." I moved impatiently, and he added, "And I warn you, if you leap up haughtily you'll fall right into my arms."

I knew that. Every drop of my blood knew it. No need to rise; I could lean forward only a few inches—

With a desperate effort I pushed myself back into the cushions, and willed my voice to come out steadily. "I'm not frightened, of course. This shouldn't be unexpected, I did seem to be asking for it."

"If I thought you were asking," said the level voice, "I might lose *all* my self-control."

"That's just it. When a girl complains that nobody loves her and suggests sitting in the dark, and then invites you—I didn't think how it sounded, but I suppose you felt the least you could do was to—to respond. Well, you've done your bit of chivalry for the night. Now you know it wasn't meant that way, you needn't—say any more."

When he spoke again there was a hint of laughter behind the low, husky voice. "I never felt less chivalrous. I wasn't paying any attention to what you said, and you've done nothing but be yourself. That was plenty."

"Barney, please. Really, you don't have to—"

"Take it easy. You're going to listen, since I've said this much already. You must have known; this has been coming on all evening, ever since I saw you there in the doorway, all done up in cellophane like something in a florist's window."

Perversely, if I hadn't wanted so much to believe him, it would have been easier; if I could ever think of myself as wine instead of water—but at least he didn't *say* zinnias.

"What a time and place I pick out!" he added with a sound that was half laugh, half groan. "There isn't time to tell you how I feel—and if there were, the set-up is all wrong. I can't say or do what I want to—

"I ask you, can I?" he said, motionless beside me in the dark.

From a great distance a voice that must have been mine faltered, "Not—now. Not tonight."

—Go on, said the treacherous small thing inside me; go on, let yourself think he means it. Perhaps this is the man you've looked for, the man who has guessed what you're really like, as nobody else has ever—

Tomorrow, I thought. "Tomorrow," my whisper echoed; and then I gave a great start.

In defiance of his own rule, Barney had caught my wrist in a hard clasp.

He was rigidly still. "Listen," he said. "Rumple up your hair, and open your dress at the collar." His breathy voice was barely audible.

"What on earth—"

"Don't argue. Do as I say. Hurry." He rose from his crouching position with a single easy movement, and crept toward the hall door.

Then I heard what he had heard: the click of metal on wood. A moment since there had been a creak from that board in the corridor. Now someone—someone with a key—was trying to enter my apartment.

I could just see around the corner into the hall. Simultaneously the hall light was briskly flicked on, and Barney, pulling the door open, said in a tone of annoyance, "What the hell?"

There was a key in the lock, and a hand was attached to it. The owner of the hand, caught off balance, fell with complete abandon into the opening, saving himself only by flinging his arms around Barney's neck. There was no mistaking the length and untidiness of that figure, even before Barney, his voice now a mixture of surprise and compunction, exclaimed, "Mr. Bassett!"

With immense dignity the figure regained balance. "Navigate under own power," our landlord mumbled, wavered into the living room doorway and touched the switch of the ceiling light.

Blinking, disheveled, looking as embarrassed as I felt, I huddled in the corner of the sofa. He raked my person with a wild and bleary eye.

"Thash what I thought," he accused me in a voice which cracked with indignation. *"Necking!"*

He steamed forward a few feet, and once more stopped dead. "Baloney," he shrilled suddenly, *"He's* no dect—no tective." I cast one horrified look at Barney, behind the landlord.

Barney's eyes were brilliant as if with a mysterious triumph.

Mr. Bassett thoughtfully lowered his voice. "Tenants, mustn' disturb other tenants," he murmured. "Thish respectable house. I'm in charge, goin' keep it respectable." He swayed a trifle from the ankles, fixing me with an implacable gaze. "Got to thinkin'. Girl went up, girl never came down again. Thought I'd come up and fin' out what's up to."

He drew in a mighty lungful of air, and I held my breath in expectation of a roar.

"Necking," Mr. Bassett said in a penetrating whisper, and sat down all of a piece on the occasional chair. Its unexpected hardness wrung from him a surprised moan.

No longer daring to meet Barney's eyes, I began to fumble sheepishly with my hair and my collar. Barney lounged over from the doorway and turned so that he faced our visitor. "Aw, hell," he said in an indefinably coarsened voice, "What's wrong with that? A man gets sick of being on the job all the time. Can't he have a little fun?"

"No," the landlord said owlishly, "no—no—no—no. Not here. I'm gonna keep place decent."

"Well, why do you have to pick on us?" said Barney reasonably. "We're not givin' any trouble, are we?"

Mr. Bassett's eyes shifted off vaguely, and he muttered with an effect of reluctant truth, "Other people all been here a long time." Then he swayed once more toward me. "You get out," he said, "ri' now. You 'n' him. Don't want immorial char'cters round here. Go on."

It struck me all at once that this wasn't entirely funny; he might mean it. Brooding among the tidies and Yards of Kittens in that first-floor lair, he had evidently arrived at this stage of pot-valiance where, Barney's threats forgotten under the anesthetic of drink, he remembered only that something was wrong in apartment 4-D.

"I'll go downstairs," he finished magnificently, "an' if you're not down in fi' minutes, baggage, everything, I'll—I'll—"

He would what? Rouse the household? Call the police to throw us out?

Barney's back was still turned to me, but he had been observing the landlord with serious attention. "Aw, look, Mr. Bassett," he said in what was almost a whine, "think it over a few minutes. It's late, and we were just—well, have a heart. Say, why don't we all have a little drink, and then talk about it?"

Mr. Bassett muttered something about carousing, but I thought the mention of a drink had touched his heart. "Sure," Barney pressed his advantage soothingly, "that's what we need. I'll get it."

He turned in the doorway, just out of Bassett's line of vision. To my startled gaze appeared a combination of gestures and silently mouthed words. "Keep him looking at you!"

I wondered madly what Barney intended to serve at this midnight feast, but my orders were clear. Mr. Bassett, wavering on his pins, was already hitching himself from his chair, presumably to meet the drink halfway. I darted into the zone of alcoholic air which surrounded him, and whispered, "Quick! While he's out of the room, listen to me."

He was still turning toward the door, and I seized his crumpled lapels. "You've got to help me. That man is a—a white slaver. He kept me up here, he said if I made a noise or tried to leave he'd kill me. You call up the police, downstairs—there's no telephone here."

"Don't want to get police—this respec'ble house," said Mr. Bassett, passing a hand over his lips and nervously trying to back away. I heard a slight clinking sound in the kitchen, and then silence.

"Oh, be quiet, or he'll hear you!" Trying not to breathe, I brought my face close to his retreating one. "You don't know what I've been through. He threatened me with—with worse than death. Listen, tell them when they come not to knock at the door. Tell them to climb the fire escape and take him by surprise." Over Bassett's shoulder I saw Barney in the doorway. "Look! Tell them to break in *that window!*"

With a dramatic gesture I released the shrinking form and swung my arm toward the rear wall. Involuntarily his eyes followed mine.

He was a little behind me. When I turned to him once more I could not believe what I saw. He was making me a deep bow.

From a distance of several feet Barney watched him solicitously.

Bassett kept on bowing, from the waist, and I stood spellbound. He bowed farther and farther, until his head was nearly on the floor. Then, without a sound, he collapsed at full length and lay there with his eyes beatifically closed.

My incredulous gaze moved to Barney. He seemed to be standing crookedly, and my look dropped slowly to his feet. One of them was bare.

From behind his back he brought out a curious object. It was a soft woolen sock, heavily and bluntly weighted. "Nice teamwork, my dear," he observed. "I was at my wits' end there, for a minute."

"What—" I began, and had to stop and start again. "What—"

"Every time I handle those cacti of yours," he said plaintively, "my hands get stuck full of prickers. I suppose, though, I ought to be thankful they were there—and growing in sand."

Feebly I repeated, "What—" like a demented sea gull.

Barney calmly up-ended his sock and dumped out the sand in a heap. "I don't advise you to make any muffins with your flour," he observed. There was a heady elation in his manner, which seemed to inspire facetiousness. "I hid the cactus plants in the flour bin. The only problem was to get Comrade Bassett's attention fixed on something so I could sock him. That was a swell performance. When you said 'worse than death,' cold shivers went up my spine."

He stood up, re-shod, and walked over to the recumbent form of our landlord. "Now what are we going to do with him?" he murmured.

"Barney, you sandbagged that poor creature?"

"Only a little tap. You have to know just where to hit; they go out like a light, and they don't wake up for a good long time. And then—they have a headache, sure, but ten to one they don't know what hit them—just like Ma Ulrichson."

"You were that worried about having the police called, or being thrown out of this building? But he wouldn't really have made any trouble, do you think?"

Barney muttered gleefully, "Walked right into my parlor. I knew staying here was the best bet. He half expected to find me snooping all over the building."

"What on earth are you doing?" I said, bending over his averted shoulder.

"Three guesses," said Barney. He was going methodically through Mr. Bassett's clothes, stacking the contents of the pockets beside him on the floor. It made a rather pitiful little heap of rubbish: a ragged handkerchief, some soiled business cards, a knife, a thinly stocked billfold and a handful of small change. Barney sat back on his heels, balancing on his palm a bunch of keys.

"Well, Fagin," I said, "what sort of company have I got into?"

"Worse than death," he replied elliptically, and grinned at me.

"You weren't supposed to hear that."

He looked up at me, the blue eyes still alight with merriment. "What a good soldier you make—throwing away your reputation like *that*. It was the only thing to do, though; and didn't it give him a jolt!"

"Wasn't it just what he expected?"

Barney shook his head. "That last of anything. Probably he thought I was out; but Lord, he's quick! He was all prepared with that drunk act, so that when I caught him at the door—"

He caught my frown, and laughed softly. "Didn't you know? Our late esteemed landlord was as sober as you are."

NINE

Closed for Repairs

"HOW DO YOU KNOW?" I said blankly.

"His hands; I was watching 'em. He did the vague stare all right, and the speech—and plonty of whisky had been spilled around—but he found that light switch on the first try."

"Look here." I stared at him. "Do you mean me to think—"

Barney got to his feet. "I can't control your thoughts," he countered in a light tone, "though you might ask yourself why he was so anxious about our movements. Let's just say—Bassett got in my way. We can't afford interference, not at this stage of the game."

I looked down thoughtfully at the limp figure. More than one sodden gentleman has crossed my path, though never in a state that had to be curbed with a sandbag. Bassett had seemed to me one of the ripest specimens I'd ever viewed.

Maybe Barney knew best; but, whether the landlord had been drunk or sober, one fact was certain. Sometime he'd wake up. This last thought seemed to echo in the mind of my companion.

"I wish I could get him put away," he said. "If there were some place where he could be locked in until I had time to deal with him!"

"Uh-huh. Picture him coming to, and me trying to handle the fireworks."

"I know— There's a lock on the bathroom, of course, but only inside. Good Lord, there must be *some* place—"

"Wait a minute." I looked up with a sudden inspiration. "That big old-fashioned key on his ring—I think I know what that unlocks."

"Give out," he encouraged me.

"On the second floor, around the corner from the staircase, there's a sort of glory-hole where Mrs. Ulrichson keeps a vacuum cleaner. She lets the tenants use it, I've seen her getting it out—and I'll swear that door has the kind of lock that fastens from the outside only."

He was already disengaging the big key. With it in his hand, he looked at me dubiously. "I'm going to have a hard time managing this alone; Bassett's no featherweight. It's asking a lot of you, Cameron, but—as long as you're with me—"

"You'll let me go along to open the door? Good egg!" He grinned at my enthusiasm. "Or shall I carry Mr. Bassett?" I added, somewhat giddy with excitement.

"Why, no," said Barney gravely. "I want him myself. Here, put that arm over my head, will you?"

He was pulling the unconscious form over his shoulder in the fireman's lift. I had a sudden vision of meeting someone on the stairs and having to explain why we were locking our landlord in a broom closet. The giggles are not a habit of mine, but I very nearly had them then. "Barney," I said, "what's going to happen in that glory-hole when he wakes up?"

"If he's got nothing on his conscience, I should think he'll bang on the door and warn us. Otherwise, he'll want to get out without any noise, without anyone's knowing—and I didn't leave a thing in his pockets that would serve to get him free."

"And as for explaining—?"

"Oh, let's work that out later. I can't think of everything at once."

I should like to have been dissociated from our next few minutes' work, and to have been able to observe it impartially and all unwarned. It must have been remarkable; the terrific creak, under double weight, of the board outside 4-B, which startled me so that I leapt an inch into the air; the processional down the stairs, me in front feeling for every step, Barney behind with his burden draped round his neck like a fox fur; the elaborate caution with which we approached the closet on the second floor, and the really bad moment when Barney had dumped his load to inspect the linen-laden shelves—and we heard footsteps on the stair coming up.

There was not really room enough for the three of us and the vacuum cleaner too; but in one second after the sound had reached our ears, we were wedged in somehow, and Barney was trying to close the door. It wouldn't quite shut, and he had to hold it while the intruder went by. I did not dare to take a breath lest the extra pressure cause it to pop open. Under our feet Mr. Bassett slumbered blissfully, his cheek pillowed on a mop.

Barney's arm across my chest was like padded steel.

And if the person who was mounting the stair should see the crack between door and frame, and the hand on the knob? What did one say—"Come right in, we're playing sardines?"

Jay, or Fingers, or Gertie—coming quietly up, on the alert for anything out of the ordinary?

It was, thank heaven, none of them. There was a rustle of silk and the scent of damp fur in the corridor, and the woman's feet tapped lightly on the carpet as she went down the hall to the right. Miss Rose Delage, perhaps, I thought; can anyone really be called Rose Delage, or are stage names customary in the business?

"Now!" Barney breathed as we heard the closing of a door at the end of the hall. I still had the key; I locked the closet and slipped the key in my pocket, and we shot up the stairs as if the whole pack were on our heels.

He had taken the other keys from Bassett's ring. Now we halted on the fourth floor, and he ventured to use the flashlight with which we had inspected the interior of the broom closet. ("If he can pick a lock with a pillowslip," Barney had said, "he's a better man than Col—than I am.") Before I had realized what he was about to do he'd pushed me inside my own door and was using the key marked 4-C, disappearing within my neighbor's apartment. I stood waiting, the blood pounding in my ears.

But there was no sound from next door, and presently he was back. "Just wanted to make sure," he murmured. I was standing by the entrance to the dressing room and he set me aside unceremoniously. "Git away from those swingin' doors, little gal," he said. "Papa's got to dress up."

Somewhere in this house two men and a woman were in hiding. I thought I knew where they had been. The ransom meeting was to take place at half-past three; it must be after two-thirty now. But if my conjecture should be right what would happen to their plans?

"Barney," I said through the crack, "those three, Jay and Gertie and what's-his-name—what if they should think the deal's off? The baby—"

He was kneeling with his back to me, bending over the Gladstone bag on the low shelf. His hand went from the pocket of the leather jacket he wore, put something into the bag—or took it out—and closed the catch. "Think of the fifty thousand dollars," he said over his shoulder. "That's their cut; they want that money. They'll leave. If the baby is with them, the boys will gang up below: if not, it'll be duck soup to get her away from Gertie."

An answer for everything, I thought. Against such confidence, the crooks wouldn't dare to pull anything unexpected.

Close to my ear a buzzer sounded, and startled me nearly out of my mind; it was the bell from the foyer. Barney was at my side, staring at his watch. So this was the signal he had been expecting!

The watch said 2:45.

The buzzer sounded again. "Five seconds between," he said. "That means they've taken Melissa with them." He was silent for a moment, staring ahead of him, calculating. Then his lips moved; he communed with himself, just audibly.

"Peterson across the street upstairs, Garwood downstairs. Jim Ferrier at the corner. If they get together in time, it's all right. But—

"I can't stand this," he said, and looked at me unseeingly. "I've got to be in on it. I'm going out there."

"Where?"

"To El Cerrito."

"The rendezvous? But wasn't Mr. Cleveland supposed to be alone?"

"I'll keep out of sight. Orders or no orders, he'll need someone. My car's downstairs—"

I moved aside silently. His hand on the doorknob, he paused for an admonition. "Lock yourself in, and don't answer the door for anyone."

"Not even you?"

"I have the key; I have all the keys, in fact. Wish me luck," he said, and without waiting for the wish opened the door and slid through.

I was left staring at the blank panels.

As if the muffled click of the lock had released a sense that had been long dormant, I had a clear and startling vision of my own conduct. Its enormity was appalling.

What I'd done during the first part of the night could be excused; but in the last sixty minutes—

I had been deliberately knocked for a loop, and the explanation offered had been a palpable lie; but I'd ignored the lie and persuaded myself that the rest was no more than an accident. I'd fought against instinct and longing to keep from throwing myself into the arms of a strange man. I'd not only seen violence and false imprisonment committed on someone else, but I had been accessory before and after the fact.

Cameron, I thought, you used to be a nice sensible girl. What does this make you?

Hurry, now, think of some more excuses. Fix up the assault and battery case, that's the worst one. Its consequences haven't come to light as yet—but they will, they will.

All right. Suppose that my wild conjecture about Bassett—the thing I had believed was in Barney's mind—should be true. If you wrenched the facts about, they could be made to fit. He was the landlady's nephew, he knew the house and its habits, he'd naturally be called in after his aunt's "accident" and could be on the spot to confer with his hired thugs.

That would explain where the baby had been taken—on the day of the accident, as soon as the manager's apartment was empty; that would be where the three kidnappers had been hiding all evening, because I knew they must have been somewhere in the house. It would clear up, too, his inexplicable support of Barney. Whether or not Bassett believed the private-detective story, he couldn't afford to refuse Barney entry; better to pretend panic and let him in, and then keep him, all unsuspecting, under close observation. Above all, that would be the reason why Bassett *also* had tried to frighten me away before I could talk to anyone about the neighbors' baby. He also knew how damaging a witness I could be.

H'm, that's better. I can almost make myself think that he's a desperate villain, and that it *was* socially correct to bop him one and lock him in a closet.

...This is *none* of I! Can this be our dependable Miss Ferris, mixed up in a melodrama with a quiet, subtle traitor known as the Cork? The Cork, who might be almost anyone, a Nob Hill socialite, or somebody at Caya's—

While I'm working at impossibilities, I'll think of Roger Tripp: Roger, who arranged this weekend for me in advance, who told me not to come back to the city until Monday, who had enough control of Caya's system to have held up any number of defense orders: Roger, who was so obviously good and innocent that any seasoned detective-fan would automatically pick him as the murderer: who had not appeared at all tonight, thus fulfilling the Cork's chief desire—to keep his own hands clean, his real identity undisclosed.

Those two theories were equally incredible.

Resolutely, I put the thought of Roger out of my mind. I had no doubt that he was as guiltless in this affair as the baby's parents, but if I pictured him as innocent, inevitably I got round to conjecturing what he'd think about *me* if this fantastic business were ever made public.

Dear Mr. Tripp, I feel almost homesick for your kind solidity. I'm very sorry I was cross when you admonished me. You didn't know the half of it, Mr. Tripp. You thought I would never choose an apartment that wasn't respectable. You said I was too sensible to take up with strange men. Are you going to be startled!

Excuses weren't any good, when I thought of that.

After awhile I walked slowly into the living room, and stood aimlessly looking about me. You know the way you feel when you've missed a train and they tell you there'll be another one in about two hours? You have to wait; you can't go home and start reading a book, because you might miss the next one too, so there you sit in the station with nothing to do but think over your past misdeeds.

The room, now that I was alone in it, looked just as bleak and impersonal as a railroad station. All the drama and excitement had gone, as if they had been sucked out the door in Barney's wake. I hadn't realized until then how compelling was the force of his personality. I'd been caught up by it, carried along—at first against my will, then, as my belief grew, in entire partisanship. He had worked hard to get me on his side, I thought; all that electric vitality, all that charm, turned on me alone.

Any woman will understand why I then went to look at myself in the mirror. Only one who has suffered from self-doubt, though, can know why I scrutinized my image so long and earnestly.

It didn't look a bit like Loretta Young.

As an experiment, I let my hair down and left it hanging free to the shoulders. No, that didn't help much; there was nothing in that rosy-cheeked and dark-browed reflection to drive strong men mad.

The deceiving voice inside me had gone to sleep, and the hard-headed, businesslike Miss Ferris was left in possession of the field. This Miss Ferris reflected somewhat grimly on the enthusiasm with which her alter ego had believed those six impossible things. It had been easy—almost *too* easy, because I'd wanted it so much.

Well, what did a girl do now? If excitement were really needed, I thought, I could always go next door and get tangled up with Mr. O'Shea.

Mr. O'Shea didn't like my presence on this scene, not one little bit. And Barney—Barney had at once known the identity of the person on the platform. Maybe the violence of my fall *had* been accidental. The fact remained that he'd pulled me down—not to save my life, but to keep me from seeing something that must remain hidden. All at once I was deadly certain of that. In spite of his partnership with Barney, I had a fairly shrewd idea of why O'Shea wanted to remain in the background of this evening's events, and why he must disappear after his work was done. It was clear that none of the principals in this affair wanted the police on the scene. Probably I was the only person in this house who would have welcomed the sight of a blue uniform.

Even Mr. Bassett, anxious for the good name of his property, would not have called them if he could help it. Mr.

Bassett, that cartoon figure with the mild, worried brown eyes and the unfortunate taste for Dutch courage—why, how could anyone imagine him as a master criminal, a gambler who staked his own freedom on the dubious chance of committing another crime and getting away with it?

"That's ridiculous," said the hard-headed Miss Ferris aloud, and stared at her reflection in the long mirror. Was I the girl who said she didn't lie her way out of mistakes? This was almost as bad.

There have been plenty of lies told tonight, though, I reflected—and remembered how nearly I myself had been taken in by Barney's incredibly convincing act, from the time I appeared in the door till the moment when I saw the note in the wastebasket. He'd said I gave him the cue myself; but with what speed he had turned it to his advantage! Quick thinking was of the essence in this affair. What was it Barney had said?—*The Cork can deal with any situation, he knows just the right attitude to take with anyone he meets*—H'm. That would almost fit Barney himself; from the beginning his manner had been a perfect blend of deference, courtesy, admiration. He knew just how far engaging effrontery could be carried. He knew exactly when to command and when to control himself—

In the last ten minutes, I told myself, I had worked up a case against three innocent persons, without a shred of proof. That came of late hours and too much thinking. Come on, Cameron, get into action. Get down your bags and unpack them.

That tall stepladder was the most unwieldy thing I'd ever tried to handle. Attempting to maneuver it in the narrow space of the kitchenette, I just missed a direct hit on the glass door of the cupboard. It hadn't looked so heavy in Barney's hands, I thought, setting it up in the hall and standing on one of the upper treads to lift the square boards from the scuttle hole.

When I dragged my large suitcase toward the opening, it scraped resoundingly on the boards. What made the room seem all at once so quiet? I stood with my head cocked for a moment, and then realized that the rain had ceased its drumming on the roof. This lull might in some measure mitigate the wild dark journey which at least four persons were making at this moment.

I tried to imagine it: the flare of yellow sodium lights on the Bay Bridge, the whine of tires on wet pavement, the damp cold of air striking through an open window. The rendezvous was to take place in a region of meadow land; for a moment it seemed that I actually saw rain-heavy grasses shining as the headlights swept across them.

They had taken the baby, Barney said; and then he'd vanished into the night, to offer some undefined help. Perhaps he was afraid that since Mr. Cleveland could no longer comply with the ransom demands, the kidnappers would discover the substitution of a worthless roll of film for the one which might have been such damning evidence. Then would something be withheld—on their side of the bargain?

I went cautiously to the big window and peered out at the side of the shade. Fog had come in on the heels of the rain, a thick mass gently shifted by the beginning of another wild wind which as yet was no more than a warning of gales to come. The alley was blurred with it, and between fog and darkness I could barely see the window of 4-B, where Colly O'Shea waited.

There must have been—I figured out later—a time when the street in front of El Central was empty. I was told that Peterson, from an upstairs window across the street, at no time lost sight of the front door of this building. Anyone who came out would at once have been sighted even in the feeble illumination of the foyer; but above the first floor the building was dimmed in fog. No one, unless he had been stationed directly below, could have heard the cautious opening of a window on the stair landing; and if a figure crept out—and upward—no one across the street could have distinguished dark clothing from a dirty gray background, nor have known which was stealthy movement of a person and which was the sullen shifting of mist. It must have happened then. There was no other time, no other way.

I bustled about in a housewifely manner, unpacking my bags and reflecting that Barney was not an expert in handling women's clothing. He'd done his best to be careful, but when this night was over I could look forward to a long session with the ironing board. In return, I made a somewhat better job of folding his clothes, which had hung in the dressing room. They might have been left there for him to deal with, but the effect alongside my things was a bit too connubial. I laid his belongings temporarily in the battered Gladstone bag.

Half past three, said the hands of my eight-day traveling clock. Funny to think that it had kept ticking away in hiding, while I searched desperately for one sign to prove my identity.

In a moment I'd tackle the carton in which Barney had placed my pillows and pictures; it was still up in the attic. Allowing myself a moment's relaxation, I lit a cigarette and stood idly contemplating my handiwork in the dressing room. Should I unpack my bags entirely or leave them here in readiness for a move back to the girls' club?

The cigarette brushed against the sleeve of a hanging garment, and the live coal, broken off, fell into the open maw of the Gladstone.

In the sort of panic that always accompanies this particular fire hazard, I scrambled among Barney's belongings. The coal must have gone clear to the bottom; I up-ended the bag ruthlessly, and dumped out a motley collection of objects, including a piece of the lining. As I found the coal and stamped on it, I observed that the inner bottom of the bag had been loose anyway. What a way to travel, with your luggage falling to pieces.

And now the things all had to be replaced. I discarded the shirt cardboards, stacked the clean handkerchiefs neatly in a pocket, and wadded the crumpled ones together. A small object had slid under the shelf, and I reached for it.

It was of tin, heavy, smooth and rectangular. I crouched there among the scattered garments, staring at the printing on the cover. An ink-pad, the kind you use for stamping—

I didn't need to open it. I knew the ink was purple.

The false bottom of the bag; a pad such as this, an uncommon object for anyone to carry around; the notes that had borne the initial C, in purple; all these things crowded together in my mind, and the hand that held the tin box was suddenly cold.

The other things went back into the Gladstone bag in a methodical hurry. I fingered each one as I put it in, but there was no rubber stamp among them. Only one more suspicious object was there: a clip of cartridges for an automatic pistol.

Now, look here, I said to myself, there may be a natural explanation for this. I don't *know* that the pad was hidden beneath the loose bottom, it might have fallen out of a pocket. Suppose he'd found it in the kidnappers' apartment, when he went in with O'Shea? Had there been some remark about a treasure trove down the cracks of a sofa? A careful search might have uncovered just such a bit of evidence as this.

But he didn't show it to me. He said nothing about it.

Well, why should he? I believed his story without this kind of proof. Maybe he'd slipped it into the pocket of the leather jacket he was wearing, and forgot about it until he dressed to go out.

—There's another motif that's been running through this whole affair: The Cork takes care to be plausible, everything that he did up to the time of the murder had a simple natural explanation—

I got up stiffly, and after a moment's thought replaced the ink-pad under the loose bottom of the bag. There was an easy way out of this perplexity. When Barney came back, I could ask him.

I've never had any patience with the ladies in the old songs, who would cast off a swain and never speak to him again because they'd seen him out with another woman. If they'd had sense enough to inquire, the woman would have turned out to be the swain's sister. Figuratively, I could demand, "Who was that lady I seen you with last night?" and—and see if his story satisfied me.

Why, how could I condemn him, how could I jump to such a conclusion after the time we'd passed together? I *liked* him—

Once more hard common sense spoke to me. It said, "You believe what you want to believe."

It would all fit! *He* tried to get rid of me, too, and then when he found I'd seen the baby he told me I couldn't go; but he kept me by a subtler method than lying in wait at the mouth of a dark alley. If Barney were the hunted instead of the hunter, he could have told me the whole story, in the very words he had used, knowing that I could check up on it later. It was all true, except for a little matter of identity; and what surer way of disarming me could he have found?

(Don't think it; you trusted him; said the treacherous inner voice, coming strongly to the fore.)

Between the two voices, and the confusion of my thoughts, I was in a whirling void of indecision; but the very measure of my doubt reminded me of how little I knew about this man, and how much he had asked me to accept on his word alone.

I'd bought it, sight unseen.

TEN

Suitable for Framing

I DON'T KNOW HOW long I stood there, nervously swinging the door of the dressing room back and forth. Closed, it showed me myself in the mirror; open, only the bleak emptiness of the hall. Once I started and looked up at the open square of the scuttle hole, willing to believe that I'd heard the crunch of footsteps, stealthily crossing the roof; but I decided that it was only imagination. Everyone was gone. I went back to my aimless swinging of the door.

My mind flicked back and forth in much the same way. Now I looked at an illusion, now into a hard and empty vista. By a simple act of will, either could seem the only reality; but the story, the background, was as solid between them as a panel of wood.

I'd not let myself say, "Barney is one of the forces of evil." I'd say *if* he were. If he were, a great deal might be explained: his careful choice of words, his refusal to look at me while he spun that engrossing yarn, his adjectives for the Cork—*diabolically clever, a brilliant organizer*; his carefully casual mention of Bassett as a possibility for the role, and then the instant disclaimers meant not quite to convince; his triumph when Bassett had blundered into the spider's parlor, offering himself as an obvious scapegoat; the restraint with which he'd only hinted at the landlord's guilt and let *me* supply the conclusion! By then, he knew how implicit was my trust.

Why, even that look of his, that half-smile which my vanity construed as tenderness, had been bent upon me at the moment when he saw that at last I believed him.

He'd spoken of danger, but the only actual danger I'd seen as yet was his own attack on me.

That talk of double-crossing might have referred to his own hirelings—the henchmen whom he'd wanted to watch, from the close vantage of a room on the same floor.

But on the other side, what part was being played by Colly O'Shea? And why, since Barney would already know that the recovered film was worthless as evidence, should he insist on its return?—Perhaps that was only a part of the story, the story he'd invented?

It was too much for me to figure out. I'd wait till he came back from that wind-swept marsh where the ransom money was even now, presumably, changing hands. Then I'd pluck up my courage and ask him what he was doing with a purple ink-pad. I'd know if the baby, that helpless pawn in this disgusting game of move and counter-move and bluff, had been safely returned. Then I could make up my mind.

Till he came back. But when would he come—if he came at all?

Presently, after a fashion, I got myself pulled together. That idea of action had worked well before; my belongings were still parked at the top of the stepladder. I'd get them down and restore the living room to its original state; then, with the oddly heartening sense that comes from being in one's own surroundings, I might be able to think clearly.

The wind was rising, for I could hear even through the roof the moan of whirling ventilators. It slackened now and again, before stirring once more uneasily over the wet roofs, down the narrow canyons of city alleys. Before remounting the ladder, I opened the kitchen window to let out the smoke and the odor of coffee that still lingered there. Up and down the dark airshaft, four stories deep, no light shone. It was nearly four o'clock—the blackest of black winter hours.

At the top of the ladder I paused before dragging down the carton of my household goods. Imagination was certainly playing tricks with my ears, for somewhere in the dim space that surrounded me a sound, murmurous and indistinct, rose and fell as if a man were speaking.

Barney's description came back to me, how he had crept over the rafters to hear my neighbors' conversation. I thought, perhaps that was only one more bit of verisimilitude to bolster up his unconvincing narrative; could you really distinguish words through these ceilings? And, it suddenly occurred to me to wonder, who was talking?

I could find out for myself, easily enough. Follow the electric wiring, he'd said, and it would guide you to a spot over the ceiling of apartment 4-B. I kicked off my shoes and took the hem of my dress between clenched teeth; thus unhampered, the crawl across the rough grid of the rafters was not too difficult, though the distance between them was as awkward as possible. A knee here, a hand reaching ahead in reconnaissance—I was approaching the source of that sound.

The low murmur resolved itself into voices, at first sounding in a quick give and take whose words were indistinguishable. Then, as with infinite care I lowered my head between the rafters, I could hear O'Shea speaking with his incongruous suavity and precision.

"I have no doubt," he said, "that you enjoy great success with women. But why did you have to keep her here—tonight?"

I should have known from that. I should have been better prepared for what was coming; but the shock was scarcely minimized. At his companion's first words a point of deadly cold touched my heart. The voice was Barney's.

He had not, after all, gone to the rendezvous—of course, he had no need to go. That had been another lie in his carefully built up structure of innocence.

What he said was, "Do you think I wanted it this way? I tried to get rid of her—until I found out how much she knew."

It might have been the echo of my own warning to myself.

O'Shea said, "A little amusement for you on the side, too."

"How like you to think of that, Colly," said Barney, and I could read nothing at all from his tone. "We'll not discuss it now. The point is, there's little danger so long as I can keep an eye on her, and that's what I mean to do—as far as possible."

"For how long?"

"Until the fireworks are over. Yes, they're sure to go off here. Jay and Fingers will come back—take my word for it."

"And I have your word that I shall have my share. But," said O'Shea silkily, "can you guarantee that your other promise will not be broken? *How much did you tell her?*"

"No more than was necessary. I told you to leave that part to me," said Barney coldly. "Don't worry, she knows—nothing essential."

He added, "You did your best to give the game away yourself."

Give the game away? The white-eyed man had been careless; then perhaps—when I saw him through the window he'd been *carrying something*.

My throat had closed until it was hard for me to breathe, but I didn't dare move or struggle for more air. The low voice, the damning words, beat on my mind like loaded whips.

O'Shea ignored that last accusation.

"And—afterward? If they asked her to identify—"

Barney laughed softly. Under other circumstances it might have been a pleasant sound.

"She'll never talk," he said, and my blood stopped circulating altogether. "I promise you that. She'll never say a word."

This was no time to faint. I had to get out of here—get back without making a sound, and climb down that ladder. If my door opened now, if either of those men saw where I'd been and guessed that I'd overheard them—my number would be called that very minute. It was bad enough now—

It was so bad that I couldn't afford a false move. I'd crawled across these rafters a minute ago without betraying my presence, but then I wasn't hampered by the dreadful weakness of terror. A creaky joint or a piece of loose plaster dislodged under my hands would give me away hopelessly.

I was moving, I'd actually managed to lever myself to hands and knees and begin backing slowly away, with painful care lowering my weight onto each support. The voices had faded to a murmur again; I must be making progress, or else the men had moved. Perhaps that had been the end of their conversation, and Barney was even now emerging into the public corridor, preparing to fit his key into my door. And then?

With inconceivable bitterness, I remembered Roger's words: "Dreadful things can happen to young women." I also remembered my inward laughter.

Is there anything more humiliating than to realize, far too late, that someone else was right and you were wrong? Heaven help me, I *needed* a caretaker. Fool that I'd been, not to wonder about my own safety!

She'll never say a word. Even a person who's been successfully duped remains a menace. Leave it to him; he'd take care of that! The dead can't talk. *You can't hang twice.*

And if he planned to kill me, what a perfect setup! Who was to bear witness that I'd ever arrived at this apartment house on the night of February 14? Nobody had seen me except the two in 4-B, and a drunken landlord who had presumably passed out after an evening of alcoholic dreams.

Sunk without a ripple; that was what they said of persons who disappeared. A woman walked out of the bus terminal and vanished like rain in the ocean.

—Here, with a shock of relief, my groping hand discovered the edge of the platform around the scuttle hole. I'd got this far, anyway. Thank Heaven for stockinged feet that made no noise on the rungs of a ladder, and for the remnant of control that made my hands lift the square of boards and fit it quietly into place above my head.

I was shaking violently when at last I stood on the solid hall floor. If the ladder could be replaced in the kitchen without disturbance, nobody need know when I'd retrieved my belongings—but I couldn't handle it now, until this trembling was subdued.

I stood there calling up the reserves, and what came to my aid was a wave of burning anger that stiffened my spine faster than a shot of whisky.

I'd been completely and handsomely fooled. How smart and cocky I had felt, trying to beat a crook at his own game instead of calling the police—and how cleverly he had played on a mind made too confident by that minor triumph! After that first failure he had changed his tactics, working conciliation and frankness and charm for all they were worth. Charm and honesty weren't inseparable, not by a long shot; some of the worst criminals in history had found it easy to enslave women.

He'd been doing all right, too.

Damn, oh, damn! How nearly I had given way entirely, how much I had wanted to lean forward those few inches when he knelt beside my chair—He'd chosen exactly the right approach, after he'd sized me up and figured that a cruder one would not do. And how much, all the time, he must have been wanting to laugh at the ease with which my defenses had fallen.

Well, by Heaven, they hadn't fallen all the way; I could still close the breach, there was that to console me.

But—he mustn't know that it was closed!

That could be thought out later. In the meantime, I had to wrestle in silence with the unhandy length of the ladder, to close it and get into the kitchen with it. With the fiendishness of inanimate objects, the ladder did nothing to help me; I tried to lower it edgeways onto my shoulder, and nearly got an ear scraped off for my pains. The thing seemed to be twenty feet long, and to have more legs and points than a swastika. Grappling with it in sulphurous speechlessness, I swore I'd never set up a ladder again, if I had to climb a knotted rope for the rest of my days.

Remove all traces— My hands and face were filthy; I scrubbed them hurriedly and brushed the plaster out of my hair. Then, with a conscious effort at composure, I turned to the mirror.

Thank goodness, I thought, rage doesn't make me pale. I looked much the same as I had looked just after he'd left; perhaps there wasn't quite the same hopeful light in the eyes—

I could hear his voice, after that first failure, saying, *You gave me the cue yourself*. And I'd gone right on doing it! I could hear O'Shea: *You enjoy great success with women*.

Of course that would be what hurt the most. I had no doubt of it either, considering how nearly I had been convinced by that little scene in the dark, the last careful touch in a masterpiece of deception. Instinct had told me that he couldn't mean it—but I hadn't had the wit to guess why it had been played. It was the only way he could get my mind off those awkward questions that were coming too close to the truth. He thought he had succeeded, too; he thought he had me in his pocket.

—And must continue to think so. That was the only way I could gain time—time to escape, somehow to outwit him. Why, that plan had worked before! I could do it again—

Things were different now. It would be harder, since in those few hours we had reached what might be called intimacy. He must see no change in my manner, I must still be his partner in adventure, trusting, thrilling to excitement, even counterfeiting the undercurrent of emotion.

Savagely I got out my lipstick and used it, needing every aid to morale that could be pressed into service. I suppose that was funny, too, only I didn't see it at the time; my hand was steady enough, but my wits were scattered, for when I dropped the lipstick and it rolled under the door on which the bed hung, I tried my best to crawl through the crack after it. A full minute elapsed before I had sense enough to go round into the other room.

I dropped the lipstick into my pocket instead of putting it away. It clinked against metal. That would be the key to the broom closet, I remembered suddenly: the closet where Bassett was imprisoned. Bassett was the one menace to Barney's scheme, and there had been no time to cajole him. He'd had to be put out of the way, immobilized, and I had helped to do it.

You have to know just where to hit them.—How could I have been so dense? That remark pointed straight to another one: *The same motif has run through this whole affair—the blow on the head.* Mangam had died of a head injury, Mrs. Ulrichson might not survive her fractured skull, the nurse Patsy Gavin had been knocked out by a rabbit punch. —Her unconsciousness had lasted only a few minutes. He'd want to be gentle with her, because unconsciously she had given him, her old friend, all the details he needed for the smooth commission of the kidnapping. Maybe they'd worked it together; who should be less likely as a suspect than a trusted employee?

But Bassett was the immediate problem. He might be too frightened and sick to protect me physically, but he was the only ally I could count on. Nobody else was within call—except Mr. O'Shea. If somehow I could let Bassett out, revive him, he could at least go for help without the knowledge of the crooks who held me as hostage. I had the key. Two long flights of stairs, one long dark corridor, lay between me and this one feeble chance.

Barney hadn't returned. Doubtless he and O'Shea, confident in the knowledge that I was meekly waiting in my own apartment, were still conferring next door. If I could get past that creaking board, I'd be safe. More than that, I realized suddenly; I could get clean away.

I didn't dare put on a coat, or look as if I were going outdoors. The corridor was dark as I slid through the door, and no sound came from 4-B. There were two spiders in there now, waiting for more flies to buzz happily into their trap. If I didn't hurry, I might meet Jay and Fingers too.

All my subconscious memory must be called into play; where was the telltale creak? I stood still for a moment and made myself remember, walk in retrospect along the red and green carpet, looking idly at the number of my neighbors' door. Yes, that was it: the board was exactly opposite the far side of the frame.

My fingers brushed along the wallpaper, struck the wood, the panels of the door. Now, one long step, let down my weight as lightly as possible—there was a faint creak like an echo of the loud protest usually given out by the board. I was past it, I was safe. Don't trip on the stair; the evidences of Mrs. Ulrichson's faked accident might still be a hazard. Third floor; third-floor landing, second floor—

Out of the darkness an arm caught me from behind, and a hand was clamped over my mouth. A wild convulsive twist was all the resistance I could make, and it got me nowhere; my arms were pinned to my sides.

The hand over my mouth moved, its fingers brushed my cheek. A whisper like a mere breath sounded in the dark.

"Cameron!" Barney said. "What are you doing here? I told you to stay—"

It was no use, no use at all; my feeble try at escape had never had a chance.

I let myself be propelled up the stairs. I'd been a fool to think I could elude his vigilance. To struggle now, or protest, would only hurry the end.

In silence we moved along the upper corridor, and came to the door of my apartment. It looked to me as if there were bars on it.

But if I could deceive my captor, with an attitude as false as his own? Now was the moment.

"You—you weren't gone long," I said, walking away from him into the lighted room.

"I didn't go across the Bay," his deep voice said soberly behind me. "There was a mix-up down below. Garwood was across the street; he saw Jay and Fingers come out of the alley and thought they were carrying the baby. The man at the corner, who could get a closer view, said no; they had a bundle, but it wasn't big enough. He let them go."

"And what about Mr. Cleveland?" I turned to face him; I had to see his expression.

"Garwood's gone out there. We agreed that I'd better stay here. —For the Lord's sake, Cameron, don't look so frightened."

"Well, I am frightened," I said. "That is, I was. You jumped at me out of the dark, and I didn't know who it was."

"I didn't recognize you either, with your hair down; might have been Gertie. It was only when I felt your skin that I knew." He looked at the palm of his hand and grinned. "First time I've ever had lipstick *there*."

Then his eyes came up to mine again, and he added, "And will you please tell me what you were doing, wandering around the halls?"

He suspects already, I thought, giddy with panic. How was I to explain—and then the one possible answer flashed like a message into my mind.

I looked straight at him, a serious look of alliance, and breathed, "I thought I heard something crying."

"Where? Not on the first floor?" His eyes gleamed from between narrowed lids.

"I couldn't tell. It was somewhere in the light well—maybe it was a cat. But since I thought you weren't here, I had to see if I could find out—"

"A cat. Probably that's all it was." He drew a deep breath and frowned. "I'd been down to make another search—in the landlord's apartment this time. No one was there. But I swear the baby must be in this building still."

I bit my lip. "You thought it had been hidden in Bassett's rooms? Maybe, if I could go in there and look around, I might be able to tell." Would he let me go? If he agreed, perhaps there'd be a chance—

"How could you tell?"

"Let's be delicate," I said, and managed a smile. "Babies do leave signs of their presence, signs that can't be seen. After you've been around them as much as I have, you can detect it."

He met my eyes, and slowly shook his head. The forlorn hope died.

"What would be the use?" he said. "Even if you thought it had been there, it isn't now. They must have got it away without our knowledge, somehow. Maybe they picked it up from another hideout. I'll have to wait and see."

I said, "More waiting?"

"Yes. Can you take it? Jay and Fingers should be back here before long. At the very least, they have to pick up Gertie."

"Sure," I said. "Sure I can take it," and smiled. This was easier than I'd expected, and now I knew why. Not to show it when you're hurt; that was the one Spartan principle my father had taught me.

"I ought to know," Barney said, and returned the smile. He did it so well! He looked so guiltless, his voice was so warm, that I was shaken by returning doubt. *Ask* him, the treacherous thing inside me urged. Who was that lady?

He had turned and gone into the dressing room. "Hullo," he said, and I imagined him stopping short, taking in the change between those narrowed eyelids. "You packed my things."

I remembered his hands, those big powerful hands, clenching and flexing. The question died on my tongue.

"Yes," I said, "just tumbled them in anyhow. I got my bags down right after you'd gone—just for something to do."

"Well," he said, returning, "I'm glad you managed to keep from being bored. I'll try not to leave you alone again."

"No?"

"No. Until the crisis comes, you'll be right under my eyes; and when it does come, I want you to stay right here. I want to know where you are—every minute from now till daylight."

ELEVEN

Lady into Fox

SHOULD I STOP HERE to point up a slight lesson? Maybe not. You can read it on the Kiddies' Page of any reputable newspaper, in one of the stories about Bad Betsy Bantam who sneaked out of the barnyard although her mommy had warned her and warned her about the big fox.

Those case histories generally end with Bad Betsy taking it on the lam back to mommy's wings, and resolving never, never, never. It looked in this instance as if I might provide a new dénouement which would send the tots to bed shrieking. I could resolve myself black in the face, but how in tunket was I to get back to the barnyard?

At that moment the shelter of somebody's wings looked like heaven on earth, and just about as attainable. In order to get so much as a head start, Bad Betsy would be forced to pretend she was a fox herself.

That'll be all about Betsy, I'm sick of her. This was *me.* And, if I was trying inwardly to be funny about the situation, it was only for the sake of courage. It didn't feel comic at all.

It's simply amazing how convincingly you can act when you're faced with an acute danger. At school when called up to recite "The quality of mercy is not strained," with gestures, I never rated more than a C; but I was getting away with this. My intuition felt as if it had been sandpapered, so that it was sensitive to the most delicate impression, and I knew that Barney did not know how much I could read into the innocent sound of his words.

From now till daylight. Was that the length of my respite? And when the dawn did come, what would happen? He'd scarcely be willing to kill me here. Perhaps a ride would be suggested: "I'll drive you to the girls' club myself, Cameron"—delivered with a smiling intimacy of look; and I'd be supposed to go with him confidently—

Maybe when the time came I could deal with that somehow. I sat down, feeling that after what had passed between us a shy reserve would be natural enough. I was even able to reflect, with a certain grim amusement, that this affair contained enough double-crosses for a game of tic-tac-toe.

If it kept up, somebody would meet himself coming around a corner.

"What happened to O'Shea?" I breathed.

"That's just the point. He's still in the next apartment, waiting. It's been a long strain, and by now he believes the worst of everybody." Barney gave me a preoccupied grin. He was still on his feet, at times standing as quiet as a jungle cat poised for a spring, at times taking a short restless prowl across the room. He glanced for the tenth time at his watch. "I heard that woman say that Jay and Fingers should be able to get back here by four-thirty, if *he* didn't meet them. Well, I believe he couldn't."

Was that where Barney had meant to go when he started on his mission, and had something happened to prevent him?

He was sitting pretty in either case. —Now he had halted with his back to me. "I wonder if we're banking too much on getting those three, if they'll be willing to talk after all. If I were they, I'd rather have the Cork for a friend than an enemy. There'd be nothing to lose if they said that there was no such person, that they'd used his name to throw people off the scent. Then we'd have to find adequate proof for what I only suspect now. It may not be easy."

I leaned back, gazing at the spread of his shoulders in the doorway. He thought of everything ahead of time. There was no doubt in my mind that Jay and Fingers and Gertie had been coached to say just that; and that, faced with their enemy O'Shea and Barney himself, they'd find that story to their advantage. I put my hands in my skirt pockets, and felt in one the smooth cylinder of my lipstick and in the other my only weapon—a big, old-fashioned key.

Barney turned. "I want you to know this," he began, "because—"

A gentle buzz cut into his words; once more someone had pushed the bell downstairs. It sounded twice in rapid succession.

"Garwood," he said. "He's back. I'd better go down and see what's happened. You come with me."

Swiftly I weighed the two aspects of this command. Did he mean it was time for our little ride, and should I demur on the ground of weariness? No, that wouldn't do. The Cameron of two hours ago would have jumped at the chance. Could I lag behind on the stair, on some pretext, and unlock the door of the broom closet?

"I'll get my coat," I said, jumping up with an eager look. I'd found it and stuffed my arms into the sleeves before he could help me. All I could do was to go along, but to stay on the alert for any chance of escape or of summoning help.

But what pretext could one use? I stumbled on one of the top steps, and he caught my arm in a firm grasp and did not relinquish it. I set my teeth in order to endure the impersonal touch, which a short while ago would have seemed comforting. We were past the second floor, and I had to wait while Barney stopped and laid his ear against the door of the closet, and gently tried the handle.

"Still in there," he murmured in my ear as we went on.

"Did you hear him?"

"No. If he's conscious, he's lying low. That sock on the head may not have laid him out for as long as I hoped; there's no telling."

Bassett might be returning to consciousness, I thought. There was a light in the closet; you pulled a long string attached to its chain. If he recovered, bewildered to find himself imprisoned, the first thing he'd do would be to pull on that light; and then, if he were to see the key lying on the floor—

There was a hundred-to-one chance in that. It might be the best I could do.

The fog had shifted and was blowing gently northward. Its stinging particles touched my face as we hurried along the wet sidewalk, down the block and around the corner to a parked car, whose dark bulk was scarcely visible until we were almost upon it.

The car window was down, and a voice spoke from within. "Hi, Barney. Here I am."

I was shoved into the front seat and wedged between the two men, and for an instant was sick with terror. The car didn't move off, though. "Miss Ferris, 's Mr. Garwood," Barney said hurriedly, in an almost inaudible tone, as he got in beside me. "What happened, Jack?"

"Washout," Garwood said gruffly. Against the window I could just make out his profile, thin and hawk-nosed.

"Where's Walter?" Barney snapped.

"Home. He wanted to come back with me, but I told him he might throw a monkey-wrench into the works; they'd recognize him too easily."

"What happened to *them?*"

"Gone. I didn't see hide nor hair of them."

"They crossed him up, did they?"

"Might have been expected, I guess," said Garwood heavily.

I sat hemmed in between the two of them, staring through the rain-streaked windshield into the thick grayed-black of the night. What did one do? Beside me, so close that I could hardly move, was Barney—playing his double role with all the finesse he had already so ably demonstrated. Anyone would have sworn that his baffled fury was genuine. He had Garwood fooled, too, and with a sinking heart I knew that my wild accusation would not stand up against his word, against the incredibly convincing perfection of his act.

If I turned at this moment to the man on my left and blurted out, "The man you're looking for is right here, in this car. *He's* the Cork, he's deceived everyone," I knew what would happen. I'd be laughed at. I'd have wasted my only bit of information.

But if Garwood could learn about it somehow when Barney wasn't there, when he was dissociated, as I had been, from the spell of that personality? He might be able to think it over, to add up evidence in sober quiet, to see the truth without prejudice or argument. And how on earth was I to get him alone?

"Well, what happened?" Barney asked presently.

Garwood told us, in terse sentences that somehow managed to convey a full and vivid picture. So much lay behind his brief summary that he and this other man and I might ourselves have been riding with Walter Cleveland on his journey through the dark, feeling the very twist of his thoughts.

I'd never laid eyes on Mr. Cleveland. It was queer that without being told I envisioned him as wearing a trench coat. That was accurate; later we knew that quite unconsciously he had taken from among his other garments this one shabby relic of World War I, tugging its belt tightly around him as he went out to face a new zero hour.

("He was early," Garwood said, "he sat there in a side street, waiting.") And we saw the baby's father, behind the wheel of a long roadster, his eyes on the dashboard clock; we saw its hands crawl to a right angle. The car backed, swung around, and slid off with a soft rush of air.

...He had been told to turn off San Pablo at a certain building, an eyeless structure which had once flourished as a night club. There it was at the end of the street, its green stucco walls wan under his headlights. To the left one block, then north again, on a boulevard roughly parallel to the Bay's shoreline.

At some moment within this hour he would be met on this road. The criminals would want, no doubt, to make sure that he had obeyed orders, that he was alone and that no one was following him. Well, damn them, he had obeyed! Let them watch from wherever they were concealed, they'd see him. —What if they wanted to make sure, let him go up and down the road for the full time, in doubt at every turn? And supposing that some stranger took a notion to drive along here during the half hour, quite unwittingly wrecking the negotiations?—Well, no use meeting those troubles until they arose.

The big car crept along, its immense power making this slow crawl as quiet as a normal pace. —There had been stories of men sent to their death, forced to walk along an empty corridor without knowing when or from what point the executioner's shot would come. Had those victims gone slowly, or had their nerves given way so that they ran, stumbling and sobbing, hoping to bring death more quickly? He had never known anything so racking as this tortoise-like pace.—Keep a close watch for the signal, a flashlight waved three times at the side of the road—

His somber, heavy-lidded eyes were fixed on the road, yet everything on either hand came into his field of vision. He saw, without consciously taking them in, small frame and stucco houses, patches of open field, a few tottering shacks set far back from the road. He could even feel a vague surprise; he had never heard of this place, didn't know it existed, and yet people actually lived here!

The road led between flat fields of waving grass; as the headlights caught those tall sheaves of green, water glistened on the blades. The rain had slackened for a time.—Luck, he thought bitterly, for the man who was waiting, somewhere along here—

A hill loomed in the way, and the road curved around it and straightened out once more. To the right, another street struck off sharply, back up the slight incline; and as he went slowly by, he thought he saw another car parked at the top of the hill. His heart began to pound unevenly. It was possible, of course, that the kidnappers were as impatient as he, that they also had been prompt at the rendezvous.

He was sure of it, when, half a mile farther on, his windshield caught a sudden reflection; a pair of headlights on the hill behind him had been switched on, off, on again. Much of the length of Panhandle Boulevard would be visible from that rise. A cry stirred in him—let it be soon, let it be now!

Here a low railroad embankment ran along the left of the road, with the faint gleam of bay water beyond it. From the right another set of tracks converged with this; he had passed the Pullman works, and a high culvert loomed up where the tracks were elevated above the pavement. Just on the other side was a great empty field. His heart gave one more dreadful leap; a light appeared, swinging up and down in the hand of a darkly muffled figure.

He stopped the car at once; the light moved away, with a gesture to the right, and he followed it up a side street, once more pausing as the glow died. The beam flashed on and off; he gathered that he was to darken his headlights, and did so.

Now, except for a dim illumination from the dashboard, there was darkness. He flicked off that light also, straining his eyes to see if the muffled shape were still in the field. There was something moving toward the car, and he twisted about in a vain attempt to follow its progress; but the figure had disappeared.

His head was craned toward the right when a voice spoke behind him. "I'm holding a gun on you, so keep still and don't turn around."

The tone was conversational, the voice an ordinary one. There were common intonations, but they were typical of a million half-educated men's voices. The father, motionless, strove to fix that sound in his mind. He could not turn his eyes far enough to see anything; at the edge of his vision the blur of dark wrappings would barely take shape, but there was an ominous click of heavy metal on the roadster's lowered window.

"You can hand out the money," the voice went on. "Soon's my partner gets here, we'll look it over."

Walter Cleveland groped beside him for the satchel, found it, and passed it over his left shoulder. A gloved hand came out and grasped the handle. "Fifty grand," the voice asked, "in small bills? No serial numbers near each other?"

"None," the father said through set teeth.

"The film's there—just like it was found?"

"Yes. Now, for God's sake!—"

"Take it easy," said the man behind him derisively.

A car, running without lights, slid up behind the Cleveland car. There was a muttered colloquy, the satchel's fastening clicked. For another long minute he waited, without stirring; then, with a breathtaking flash of hope, he saw a man stumbling away from the car, through the grasses of the field, with a small bundle in his arms: laying it against a fence, far back in the meadow, coming back briskly.

The first man spoke once more. "When I give the word, you get out of your car," he commanded. "We'll take it up the road a mile or so, so's you can't run after us too fast—not that *that'd* be any use. But we'll leave it in an alley behind them buildings up there, on account a hot car ain't going to help us none."

The engine of the other car started up, it swung out ahead of him—useless, in this darkness, to attempt a glimpse of the license, but the car looked like a Chevrolet sedan. "Now, okay!" the voice prodded him. "Out the far door, and keep your back turned."

His jaw clamped shut in helpless, bitter rage and shame, he obeyed, his eyes on the picket fence across the meadow. Both cars were far up the street in a moment, their lights going on at a safe distance. He was running, stumbling, threshing through wet tall grass, groping along the ground by the fence. His hands touched a soft bundle, and then, shaking, felt for a lighter and snapped on the tiny, wavering flame.

There were Melissa's bunny coat and hat, a few other pieces of baby's clothing, wadded and wrapped up to simulate a small form: nothing else. The lighter dropped into the wet grass and was extinguished.

After a time the father got up stiffly, gathered the garments in both hands, and plodded back across the field. For a merciful space he had felt entirely numb in body and mind; no anger at this ghastly trickery, no pain, no thought of what to do next, had made a way into his consciousness. At this minute, for some reason, only one thing seemed important; he had to know the time. There was a match pack in his coat pocket, and he began to strike matches methodically, trying to shield them from the wind long enough so that he could turn his watch to the light. That was how Garwood found him…

"Standing in the grass, striking matches," Garwood said. "He looked up at the car lights, and his face—"

Barney had neither spoken nor moved, but against my side I could feel his quick heavy breathing. Why did he keep his face averted, staring through the car window, unless he was afraid of showing triumph? His plan had come off, he was safe; no one would suspect him now.

That was why he'd had to play it out, pretending he still wanted the film pack: because only he knew it was worthless. He must pretend caution to the end, because too easy an acceptance of terms would give him away—

"We thought of it after they left, of course," said Garwood, "when Jim told us the baby was still in the building. The film was the important thing. Those two men haven't come back yet. You want to bet they're looking at the negative right now, to make sure?"

"That's it," said Barney harshly. "I should have foreseen it. The Cork wouldn't leave anything to chance."

He wouldn't, if he were a stranger. Play it in character, Barney, you're doing fine. String us along until you're sure you'll be safe. You didn't count on one thing, though—on a little trip I took over the rafters.

I sat hugging myself, trying to shrink into the smallest possible space, but acutely aware of physical contact. Barney's arm lay across the back of the seat, behind my shoulders, and in the crowded space his knee touched mine. On the other side my hand brushed the folds of Garwood's loose overcoat.

In the right-hand pocket of the overcoat was a folded paper, stuffed in so carelessly that it was about to fall out.

Paper, I thought, and my mind offered an instant translation: message. —If I only had a pencil! My right arm, crossed so that the hand was out of Barney's sight, was free to work the paper out of Garwood's pocket and lay it against my thigh. But what could I use?—I didn't dare search farther into the pocket for something to write with—

Lipstick. Lipstick, in my own pocket.

I had to put my hands in my lap for a moment, since it took both of them to screw the stick of paste into the top of the container. That was the worst moment, though I could have pretended to be nervously fiddling with it. Barney's head was still turned away, though, and I got my arms crossed again and felt the paper under my fingers.

"Barney is the Cork," was what the point of the lipstick traced across the fold of paper. I couldn't look at it; there was no telling how legible the message might be. No more could I guess when Garwood might see it; and, if he should happen to find it within the next few minutes, would he have sense enough to recognize it as a secret communication? I had to take the chance.

He didn't notice when I slid the paper back into place. Barney had rapped out, "The boys are still watching? They'll signal?" and Garwood said yes.

"There's a chance. Jay and Fingers may feel they're safe now," Barney muttered.

Garwood said heavily, "But they still have Melissa. Have you thought what may happen when—when they do discover that they're caught?"

"I've thought of it. Gertie and the child vanished into thin air after the other two left. I searched all three of those apartments, and she wasn't in any of them. We'll get the men, with any luck, but she's still at large. That means we have to work fast."

His shoulder jerked suddenly. I hadn't realized that he was keeping a close watch on the dark reaches of the street, and it was only by chance that I saw, far down at the next corner, a point of light that winked on and off, on and off.

"Somebody coming," he said, and was on the sidewalk before either of us could reply. Garwood pushed me toward the door, and when I was nearly out of the car Barney picked me up at arms' length and swung me half across the walk. We were running toward the front door of El Central with such haste that I seemed to be carried along between the two men.

"They'll make for the alley, most likely," Barney's words jerked out almost as fast as he was moving. "That's the way they came out, tradesman's door—next to Bassett's back entrance. I'll stay there. Jack, you take—front. No noise if you can help it. Don't want to—wake up the house."

We had reached the foyer, and he gave me a shove toward the staircase. "Get up there, Cameron, into your own apartment. *Run.* If O'Shea tries to interfere, tell him we're bringing them up. Shut your door and *don't come out.*"

I went. He had flattened himself against the wall in the darkness of the rear entry, and was watching me, listening to my feet on the stairs. Garwood was staying there, too; no chance to get him alone.

That part of my brain that was functioning clearly under the swirling waves of panic told me what I must do. The key, it said: the door, round the corner to the right in the second floor hall.

He'd still be listening. Deliberately I tripped on the top step of the first flight, and fell full length. It was just possible to reach the door of the broom closet with an outstretched arm. I felt for the crack, and slid the key through it; it rasped across bare boards inside.

I could have sworn I heard a slight answering movement, but there was no time to lose. I was on my feet again, hurrying up the two remaining flights and gaining sanctuary in my own room.

The brain had not functioned quite long enough. Not until I was standing breathless behind the closed door did I realize what would have been a better move; I should have dodged aside into one of the dark upper halls and waited there until those two and their captives had gone past; then it would have been easy to return.

And now it was too late. Even as I reached the third floor, abnormally sharpened hearing had registered the opening of a door below, and the sound of muffled movement. I turned out the lights in my apartment and waited, my ear pressed against the door-panel.

They were coming. There was little need for caution now, for footsteps were plainly audible in the corridor, the steps of four men at least. They made a confused, shuffling noise as if some of them were reluctant to move.

The board outside 4-B creaked loudly, and I heard a door open.

Not the least fantastic feature of this incredible night had been the silence, the lowered tones in which everyone had spoken. My own voice had scarcely reached a normal pitch since the first moment when I'd opened my door and walked into a nightmare. Now, for almost the only time, I heard a loud noise.

It cut through the stillness in a dreadful shriek of despair. I hope I never have to hear a sound like that again; it was the voice of one who has thought himself safe from a just but terrible punishment, and who has come suddenly face to face with the executioner.

"Colly!" it said. Then the door closed, and silence came down once more.

Shaking from head to foot, I stood there listening. There was no sound in the next apartment now. I couldn't imagine, I couldn't let myself try to think, what was happening to those two wretched criminals who had been dragged in there. I remembered only that Colly O'Shea had been promised revenge. Would he have it before or after they had been questioned?

For half a second I wondered why the Cork should turn over his own associates to their enemy; the part played by O'Shea puzzled me more than anything else.—But there could be any number of reasons for that; this could be the Cork's way of insuring their silence, or another play to the gallery.

There wasn't time to figure it out. In the grip of my obsession I could think only that I had to do something—something to outwit the man who had so cleverly and unmercifully used me, to turn the tables on him.

And I was helpless.

It was so still! I could have sworn that no one was awake in the whole apartment house, or for blocks around. The whine of wind in the light shaft, which had been so loud when last I was alone here, had died also; no rain had fallen for an hour, so that even the drip of moisture outside the windows was stilled. You get moments like this sometimes, in the midst of a winter storm. They make you feel that the elements are holding their breath, gathering strength for another onslaught.

It's queer to look back on that now, and realize how much depended on those few minutes of quiet. Depended—that's the right word for it, because as I stood in the dark hall I felt that everything around me was hanging by a spider thread, motionless between sky and earth. It didn't seem right to breathe. My pounding heart, which a minute since had been almost audible, quieted to an imperceptible throb.

Then I heard it. I couldn't believe my ears at first. I'd lied about that sound before; was I imagining it now, had I thought it into being?

Just as I had described it, the noise might have been made by a cat—but I knew it wasn't.

Somewhere quite near me a baby had given a single muffled wail.

TWELVE

Doubled and Vulnerable

YOU KNOW, UNTIL THAT moment I hadn't actually thought of the baby as real. Yes, yes, I'd heard her and seen her and heard a description, I'd felt a normal bitter loathing toward the kidnappers; but from the dramatic aspects of Barney's story she'd come to seem more of an object, a symbol, than a human being. She was something to be bargained with, to be searched for and saved. Now for the first time I was in touch with reality.

That small stilled wail might have come from Sandy Crosley, waking up sick and feverish and wanting someone to come to him. How many times I'd been roused from sleep by just such a sound—a sound inaudible to the ears of anyone who hasn't cared for children!

But where was the baby that I could have heard her so plainly? For an insane moment I thought she must actually be in my apartment. I stood still, trying to remember from what direction the cry had come. Then I heard it again, and heard it abruptly cut off.

The kitchen window was open. Going toward it on silent feet, I could see into the light well. My kitchen and that of 4-C were side by side, and both looked into the well from the north; the bathrooms of the two, on east and west, faced each other across the deep shaft, at right angles to the kitchen windows.

The gray of a coming dawn filtered through the blackness, just enough so that I could see the bathroom window of the next apartment. It also was open about six inches from the bottom.

While I stared at it the frosted glass was brightened with a diffused light, seemingly from a lamp in a hallway. Someone had come hurriedly into the bathroom, and that person was leaving now, for the light faded. The baby did not cry again.

Gertie, I thought; and what's she doing to that frightened little scrap? She won't let the baby get noisy, surely.—I've got to get in there somehow! No matter what else comes out of this, the child's life is the important thing.—

And there was nobody I could get to help me. I had left one message in the hands of a man who might not find it for hours, if ever. I had given the means of release to another who for all I knew was still unconscious, and who couldn't be reached in any case. Next door were four men who wished for my silence. The newspaper reporter was somewhere, but how was I to call him away from the others? In that moment I distrusted even him; I had only Barney's word, notoriously worthless, that Garwood was what he seemed.

No need to point out that I wasn't thinking very clearly. In the haste and panic of those minutes all I knew was that I had to play a lone hand. There was no time to lose.

O'Shea had said something, all those hours ago, about inspecting 4-C from the front. The fire escape on my side, the rear of the building, led to the roof via a straight ladder. I'd never consciously noticed the escape on the front, but there was every reason to believe that it was similar. If I could get out, past the window of 4-B, and cross the roof, I might be able to surprise the woman and—and do something; I didn't know what.

Get in there somehow; get into the Spelvin apartment.

A cold touch of reason told me that Gertie would have locked the door, to which Barney held the extra key; and that if she had any sense she'd lock the window onto the fire escape also. Never mind, perhaps I could break it in.

I was across the living room, this idea firmly fixed in my head before I had time to evaluate it. Thank goodness, the big window had been oiled, so that it went up quietly. I slid out onto the iron platform.

The bay window of 4-B was also open, the merest crack, and light shone dimly through the shade. A voice was speaking inside, babbling on a breath of pure terror. "I don't know," it said hopelessly. "I tell you I don't know, I don't—"

The shade jerked up as I came abreast the opening. It was not possible to see what went on inside, for Barney's broad shoulders blocked the whole window. He'd heard me—

"Get back!" he said savagely. "Get back in your room!"

Half sobbing with frustration, I obeyed. I couldn't get out that way. I couldn't tell him what I had heard or where I was going; let him think I'd come only out of curiosity—Heaven send he didn't suspect I was trying to escape.

Through the corridor? On the front of the building the fire escapes could be reached through windows in the stair landings. I had little hope of that, for my enemies were keeping a close watch. Nevertheless I eased my door open and looked out.

Barely visible at the top of the stairs a man waited. In the darkness all I could see of him was that he was slender. Of all the people I did not want to meet, the chief was Colly O'Shea.

There was no other way to get out. I thought desperately, in a movie Roger Tripp would miraculously have guessed that I needed help, or Mr. Bassett would have recovered, escaped, called the police. They'd come charging up the stairs just at the right moment. But this wasn't on the screen; this was me, myself, trying wildly to get out of an impossible situation.

I could have yelled "Police!" down the light well, as I had threatened to do a long time ago, before I had fallen under the spell of brilliantly handled propaganda and had begun to believe what wasn't so. But such a cry would warn not only my enemies but Gertie.

If I could only step across those few feet of space in the well: ten feet or less separated my bathroom window from the one facing it, the one that had been left so temptingly open. There had been no need for Gertie to lock that one. She would remember the distance that seemed so small and that not even a giant could span. She would be made confident by the sheer drop of four stories to the bottom of the shaft.

Wasn't there any way? I stood clenching and unclenching my hands in a rage of frustration, staring out into the dimness of the well. These windows were only about two feet wide, but I could get through the bottom half of mine. And then? Craning out, I saw that the kitchen of 4-C was tightly closed. There was a rickety drainpipe on the wall between, but even if it would support my weight I doubted that I could hang there long enough to force open the kitchen window beside it; and there would be noise—

The bathroom, at right angles. Right angles—the sum of the squares of the sides of a triangle—

If I had something to use for a bridge, if I could creep across to that open window—where was there something long and flat, and stout enough to hold me up? The ironing board wasn't fastened to a fixture, it was something like that I needed; but it wasn't long enough, only about five feet. Something much taller than I, to stretch across the hypotenuse.

There was a ladder.

On a wild surge of hope I swung around, measuring its height with a calculating eye. Length overall, eight feet or more, I thought. It might do; just barely, it might do.

Maybe if I pushed the ladder half way out the window, I could gauge its length—no, that wouldn't be safe; I had to *know*, for I could not risk the danger of dropping it if it should prove too short. I should, for certainty, measure it and the distance—and I had nothing with which to measure, nothing but a tape in my sewing basket, up in the rafters. There wasn't time to climb up for it, nor would it do me any good, since I dared not turn on a light.

Well, *think*, I challenged myself. I knew how tall I was. I knew how far my arm would stretch above my head, because at home there was a cupboard shelf seven feet above the floor, and I could get my fingers over the edge of that. The ladder's top platform was possibly a foot above my normal reach.

In a solemn frenzy I measured my length on the kitchen floor, the top of my head pressed against the wall. The door jamb struck midway up my shin, which meant that the kitchen wall was about four and a half feet; the well, then, was a bit more than nine feet across. Allow two feet to the edge of the window, maybe two feet to the bathroom window in the right-angle wall—seven square plus three feet plus four feet—oh, thunder, what a time to go horsing around with mathematics! How did it go? Square of the hypotenuse—yes, that was it; equal to the sum of the squares of the sides.

Madly gabbling to myself in a whisper, lying down and scrambling up again, reaching as far as I could up the side of the ladder and mopping sweat from my brow between times, I looked like a top candidate for the loony bin; but I got it. It came out near enough, anyway, that I could afford to try pushing out the ladder.

There was a bit of leverage formed by the windowsill and the top of the cabinet. Panting, growing blazing hot, I managed to slide the unwieldy thing partially through the window and point it toward the opening. It must be held firmly; I had to lean far out to support it when its center had passed the point of balance. The wood scraped along the windowsill, and I gritted my teeth; the sill should have been padded, but I couldn't let go now. The square of the hypotenuse is equal to the sum of—You didn't foresee this, Cameron, when you yawned over your algebra at school. You taught the young to develop their muscles in gym, but you never thought that all your strength would be needed—not like this.

There was one horrible moment when I thought I should have to let go, and in anticipation I could hear the crash, the cracking of wood far below the window. Then the platform end of the ladder touched the wall. One more lift, and it was over the sill, securely hooked, and balanced at my end.

But it balanced only on one side. On the outer edge, the slope of the sill fell away from under it; the least weight would tilt the ladder sideways.

I was muttering under my breath, and to this day I don't know what I said, curses or prayers. I hope the good Lord accepted it as a cry for help, no matter how it was phrased. Something helped me; something made me think of the ironing board, which could serve as a prop if it bridged the space to my own bathroom window. I could press it into service. Press the ironing board: *ha ha*, I thought dizzily; *very funny*.

The dizziness served as a merciful anesthesia over that part of my mind which might have thought of consequences. Physically I was keyed up far enough to have started out walking on air; I didn't hesitate, once the bridge was anchored, to kick off my shoes and tuck my dress skirt into its own belt. I'd need all the freedom of movement I could get.

There was one more bad moment. Poised on the sill, I thought of the day I'd set cup custards to cool in the window, and had knocked one of them off. It had fallen—oh, heavens, how long it had taken to reach the bottom of the shaft, while I watched from above with a fascinated interest. The smash of broken crockery had come up only faintly to my ears.

This won't do. Come on, get out onto the hypotenuse, don't stop to think how narrow it is. Yes, it will bear your weight. It's solid enough at both ends. Nobody's heard you, nobody knows what you're doing.

And *start*, put your knees on the nearest rung and reach forward for a hold on the next one. That's what you did when you were creeping across the rafters; tell yourself that what's below you is only a shallow hole full of plaster, not—not a black void, not an emptiness—

Think of the recipe for cup custard. Two eggs, two tablespoons of sugar—Consider what o'clock it is. Consider what a great girl you are. Keep putting your hands ahead, holding tight even if the treads of the ladder dig into your knees. Don't look down, whatever you do. Pretend you're nearsighted, and look only at the rectangle of that half open window, coming nearer, nearer—

There were only eight rungs to the ladder, after all. It can't have taken me more than a minute to make the journey, to feel the solid sill under my groping hand and thrust head and shoulders inside the opening, pushing gently upward until the window rose with the faintest of creaks and I could wriggle inside. Getting in head foremost was part of the job I hadn't counted on, but it was made easier than I deserved by the discovery under the window of the radiator, and an end of the bathtub beside it. Once more I could have screamed with thankfulness to find solid floor under my feet.

I was in 4-C, and nobody had heard me. With some surprise I realized that the storm's breathing spell was over, and the wind was tearing over the housetops once more, driving in a new detachment of pouring rain. I turned toward the door of the bathroom, and felt a damp wad of cloth under the stockinged sole of my foot. Gertie must have left the baby in here, or brought her in to change clothing.

I would not look again at the window, nor at the ladder.

The apartment was dark, but as I eased open the door of the bathroom I thought there were sounds of stealthy movement in the main room, and once a little gasping cry. Gertie wouldn't have made a noise like that. —She has her orders, I thought. Maybe she wouldn't kill the child unless it became strictly necessary; but she has to keep it quiet.

The door to the living room was ajar. The shades were down on the front windows, but just enough dim light seeped through them to let me make out the woman's figure. The chesterfield was between me and the windows. She was bending over it, her back to me.

Some power quicker than mind, stronger than conscious will, pushed me forward. I was across the room before I fairly knew it, and had pounced upon the stooping woman, crooking one arm around her neck, snatching for her hands with the other. She came up with a choked grunt of surprise, and something dark and soft flew from her grasp and struck the floor behind me. A pillow—she'd had a pillow over the child's face, pressing it down—

For a brief second I had the advantage of a surprise attack. Then my captive began to fight, with the terrible strength of panic. Her body straightened with a vicious lunge, and jerked forward until my hold nearly broke. Gertie's foot caught under an edge of the carpet and she went down, carrying me with her. The thud sounded as if it would shake the building, and in a vague recess of my mind a thought registered: we'll be heard, someone will come to help her. But nobody came, and she writhed under me without a sound, flailing wildly behind her with ineffectual arms.

But of course; she couldn't cry out, because my forearm was still pressed against her windpipe. Now we were on our feet again, somehow, and she was trying to drag me across the room. With a sudden twist she wrenched herself half free and launched a kick backward.

Her hard shoe-heel caught me on the knee, sending a crackling wave of pain through my whole body. Gertie, seizing her advantage, brought the heel down with a cruel stamp on my foot, and almost succeeded in loosening my grip on her wrist. We were in the middle of the room now, locked together, staggering to and fro, and she knew where I was most vulnerable. I had to twist and sidestep to escape another vicious lash from her heel; her mop of long-bobbed hair dangled temptingly in front of me, and I wound a hand in it and jerked violently. The woman's head came back with a faint moan of pain, and she dropped suddenly to the floor.

I was caught off balance and pulled down beside her; and Gertie, with a great heave and twist, flung me aside and was up, free, blundering toward the hall door.

Sick and giddy with pain, I couldn't have got up for anything on earth. All I could do was to reach out feebly and grasp her ankle as she went past.

I heard a nauseating sort of thump; and then, for the second time that evening, the sound of a body slumping inertly to the floor beside me. The ankle was still in my grasp. For a moment I lay there stupidly, holding on tight but totally unable to figure what had happened.

For that moment there was no sound in the room but my own labored, sobbing breaths. Then I became vaguely aware of a little stir on the couch behind me, and the faintest peep of a voice.

The baby wasn't dead.

I think that for the last few minutes I had believed Gertie a murderess. That's the only way I can explain the surprise, the numbing shock of relief, that I felt at hearing the small voice of Melissa Cleveland. She's crying, I thought, and Gertie doesn't care; what's the matter, why doesn't she get up and do something? I couldn't stop her.

Then a slight ripple of sense stirred my mind, and I hauled myself painfully to a sitting position. Gertie lay there, out like a dead mackerel. Conscientiously I began feeling over her in the dark, and she didn't stir. Groping about her head, my fingers touched the leg of a table, then the mass of frizzy hair, and then her temple; from the last they came away wet.

So that was it: a fall, the corner of a table, unconsciousness. Sheer luck, I added vaguely. Luck, and the final blow on the head of this affair, which had been so monotonously concerned with head wounds.—But I didn't intend it, I thought, sitting stupidly on the floor; and was shaken by meaningless, helpless laughter.

The baby peeped again, a forlorn little breath of sound. I brought up a hand to my aching head. Things were clearing, slowly, and the terrible pain in my knee had subsided to intermittent pangs. Maybe I could get up in a minute. Why, yes; I'd have to! This was only a waypoint to victory.

Gertie stirred, and gave a choking moan. All at once I came to myself. Good grief, I couldn't throw away a chance like this! She was *hors de combat,* but she wouldn't stay that way long; and if I left her, it wouldn't be many minutes before she could call for reinforcements.

Blindly staggering to my feet, I thought that rope was what I needed—good strong thin rope. And where would one find that? The next time I'd bring some with me.

And presently, still half unconscious, I found myself in the kitchen, groping in the dimness for a dishtowel: then back in the living room, kneeling beside the woman and stuffing the towel into her mouth, tying another tightly about her jaw. I never bound and gagged anyone before in all my life; somehow the situation hadn't arisen. I had to do the best I could on instinct, and with makeshift material such as Gertie's stockings.

—I hope they're her best chiffon ones, I thought, and again rocked weakly with idiotic laughter. The brain was definitely affected, though little by little improving; but my hands, shaky as they were, knew what to do: pull the woman's arms over her head, fasten her wrists to the leg of a heavy chair, and lash her ankles to the bar of the table. That ought to hold her—if I haven't tied granny knots by mistake. This will puzzle them at Scotland Yard.

And still nobody came.

Why, I was free! I was going to get out of this mess, and take the baby with me; all I had to do was open the window and climb down the fire escape to the street, and then run—run anywhere, to light and safety and someone who'd help me—the police—

The child made a soft heavy bundle in my arms. She must have been sick and dopey still, because she made no other sound after the despairing cry that had roused me from stupor. I could hear her breathing, though. The blanket in which they had wrapped her was damp, and the small face and hands were cold.

I opened the window and stepped out into a fury of lashing rain.

I had forgotten so many things: I had not remembered that the fire escapes didn't go clear to the ground, and that to all intents I was still trapped in the building. Crawling step by step down the iron stairs, painfully because the bars seemed to be cutting through my unprotected soles, I had to revise my plan of campaign. Alone, I might have hung by my hands and dropped that comparatively short distance to the sidewalk. With the child, it couldn't be done, and no more could I leave her on the steps, exposed to a soaking downpour, while I went for help.

I peered up and down the dim reaches of the street. There was not a soul in sight; not one of the reporters who had been on guard earlier, not a milk wagon, not a single person who'd hear a call. Moreover, any of my enemies, prowling through the halls and staircases, might see me as I went past the landing windows. Pausing for breath where the blank wall sheltered me, I thought, "*That's* where Gertie hid while the three apartments were searched. She waited out here until the searchers had left, and as soon as they cleared out of the Spelvin apartment she ducked in there."

Yes, and here was the window from the staircase landing where she must have crept out, after Jay and Fingers went to the rendezvous. Possibly there was too much disturbance in the halls, she didn't want to risk meeting anyone; there'd be only the first flight to negotiate after she left Bassett's apartment. No, she couldn't have been in there. That had been only my own silly theory. Where *had* she hidden? Oh, what did it matter?

I got in the window. Everything was quiet in the dark halls, and on a venture I crept up the half flight to listen at the door of the broom closet. There was no sound from within; the door, when I tried it, was still locked.

Then Bassett could not have awakened. He was in there yet, sleeping off his binge, and my maneuvers with the key had been in vain.

Well, no matter. I had outflanked the enemy now, and without their knowledge I was facing a clear track. The door was open to the street and freedom.

But what did one do about the baby—take her out in this frightful storm? She was chilled already, and I hadn't so much as a jacket to wrap around her. If I could only get to a telephone, I thought; call the police, and the Cleveland family, and an ambulance! Presumably all around me were tenants, sleeping peacefully, each with a telephone for making business appointments; and I didn't know one I could trust, nor did I have an idea of how to arouse them without making a commotion that would call the pursuit from the top floor. I did not dare to linger in the darkness of these corridors, for at any moment someone might go into my apartment and find that I had got out. And yet, what did one do about the baby?

But of course, I reminded myself wearily, Bassett's apartment—if I can only get in. It will be warm and sheltered at least, and I can wait there until the police come.

The door to the hall was locked. I had expected that, and I knew when I pressed the bell-button that nobody would answer. It was done only for form's sake, because I had another idea how I might get in. From some unexpected source of memory, I had dredged up a picture of the manager's back door, the one opening on the alley beside the tradesmen's entrance. Once, looking down Mrs. Ulrichson's inner hall, I had seen that door; it had a glass pane in the upper half.

I was out in the alley, stepping carefully on the slimy dampness of the paving and feeling about me for a loose piece of rock, before I thought that Jay and Fingers had presumably intended to get in by this rear entrance—No, that couldn't have been it, unless they were in collusion with Bassett, and of course that was not so. My head wasn't very clear yet. I shook it impatiently, and on impulse tried the door.

It was unlocked. Shucks, I thought with a suddenly light heart, there goes my chance to break a pane of glass with a brick; I've always wanted to do that. Anyway, here's a stroke of luck at last. After all that terrible business with the ladder and Gertie, maybe I have this coming to me.

And we were inside, moving through the dark and unfragrant entry, coming into the dingy living room where the light from the bead-fringed lamp dazzled me with its brightness. There were the tidies, there the Yard of Kittens (and what, I wondered, would Mr. O'Shea think of *that?*) and there, thank Heaven, was the telephone.

Here in my arms was Melissa Cleveland, aged eleven months.

I had my first look at her as I stood there, savoring momentarily the exquisite feeling of safety. Her small face was pinched and pallid and the auburn curls above it draggled, but I could see how sweet she was, how she must have been loved and petted. As I looked, she stirred in my arms, and seemed to find them experienced in holding babies, for her head turned to nestle against my shoulder.

"Poor little frog," I said under my breath, "it won't be long now. You'll have your mother."—Had there been times when she waked to full consciousness, and was frightened and bewildered at the strange hard faces around her? How had they drugged her—by mouth, or by plunging a needle into a shrinking small arm?

And who would be punished for this crime, against a child so young that she could never strike back? Jay and Fingers might suffer for it, and the woman who held the pillow over the baby's face; but I wanted complete justice—complete, to include the man who had planned the whole hideous affair in a last gamble to save his skin. He might get away with it, too, if it weren't for me.

In a last minute access of caution, I turned a big chair to the wall and carefully laid the child down so that she was invisible from the rest of the room.

This was a moment to savor. "I'm the only one who knows who the Cork is," I thought; and in the intensity of that hatred heard the words come out aloud, in a stage whisper that seemed to fill the quiet room. Push me around, would he! I'd get to the police first and tell them my story, and let them and the Cleveland family settle with him.

For one moment I hesitated, nevertheless; then I thought, with a wry grin, "Service to your country—incidental to everything else!" and stepped forward to the telephone.

I dialed at once, in a single sweep of the "0." All you had to say was, "I want a policeman." In a few minutes the whole thing would be over.

The telephone was on a long cord—a very long one which seemed to reach clear into the bedroom. I held the transmitter close to my ear, waiting for an answer. Something was wrong. Shouldn't it have buzzed when I picked it up?

"You can put that down," said a soft voice behind me.

THIRTEEN

Forfeit to the Dawn

I KNEW, OF COURSE. Actually, I had known for minutes past, and had refused to face reality; the blindfold had been slipping from my eyes and I'd snatched it back deliberately—the thick muffling fabric of my own hurt vanity, that I had felt myself bound to use.

Slowly, I faced about and saw what I knew I should see. In the bedroom doorway Mr. Bassett stood, quite sober in spite of the aroma which hung about him still. There was nothing wavering about his outlines now, and no trace of unsteadiness in the hand that held, pointed at my breast, a small but businesslike revolver.

His face looked different, too. The yellowish pallor which I had seen before had faded to a dead white; and, by some trick of taut facial muscles, his eyes seemed to have receded into his skull. From their sunken caverns they looked out at me, inhumanly bright.

The face and the eyes were those of a fanatic, who in the necessity of defending his deeds had pressed forward from venial sin to crime to more dreadful crime, until at last nothing was left but self-defense at any cost.

"Put it down," he repeated in that far-off voice.

I looked at the dead telephone in my hand and replaced it in its cradle. A minute since I had voiced my thoughts aloud, and I knew he had heard me.

It was a curious thing that I was not in the least frightened. Maybe I'd been scared so thoroughly and so often that night that I was at last immune; but all I felt was rage, with myself and him—and, coupled with it, a sudden icy clarity of mind.

"You can't get away with any violence, Mr. Bassett," I said quite loudly. "You know what will happen if you shoot me. The sound of the shot will bring a dozen men here before you could get away."

"Oh, but I don't want to shoot you—not in this apartment," he said, in a tone that was dreadfully reasonable and polite. He was pleased with his mastery of the moment. "A shot's my last resort, if you try any tricks. Maybe it'll make things tough for me, but by that time you'll be dead."

I shook my head, staring at him contemptuously. "It won't work at all. You forget that Barney has suspected you from the first. No matter what I said, I'm not the only one who knows the identity of the Cork. He knows it too."

Bassett actually smiled, but with his mouth only. The sunken eyes gleamed steadily, their expression unchanged. "What does he know? He knows he's got someone shut up in that broom closet, a man who might be the Cork—but he can't prove a thing on that man. The Cork! There's a damn fool name for you, trust the newspapers to think up something like that. But the closet's locked. Nobody saw me come out, and nobody'll see me go in again. I'll have a perfect alibi, and that rat you call Barney will have given it to me himself! I can lock the door on the inside and nobody'll ever find the key where I'll hide it."

"And your hired crooks? Don't you think they'll talk?"

"They want me alive and free to help them." His pale tongue came out and licked once around his lips. "I'm not afraid they'll sing. Come on. We're wasting time here. You walk ahead of me into the alley."

"Like hell I will," I said. "Go on, shoot. You care more for your safety, right at this moment, than for anything else. You don't dare make a noise."

"How right you are, dear Miss Ferris," said Mr. Bassett with loathsome geniality. "How cleverly you think things out. You slipped up just once this evening, when you let me out of the closet. Well, I owe you something for that. I'll give you a chance to save the kid's life."

Then he knew she was here. The little creature hadn't moved nor made a sound. He must have been watching while I laid her in the chair—

"The kid's little," he said agreeably. "I could choke her with one hand, and hold the gun on you with the other. Then, even if you knew I was going to be caught, what good would it do you? You'd die knowing that her death was your fault. Okay, you can save her if you mind what I say."

There were no dissentient voices in my brain now. At last it was integrated, and it told me clearly that he was right, that a child's life was the greater, more immediate stake. If only I could stall him a little longer! The men might come from upstairs at any minute—

But he had foreseen that, too. "Pick her up," he said, "and take her with you. You think I want her found here? You can lay her down outside. Don't get excited, you're not going to be saved, you'll be too close to the point of my gun."

I thought, *"Barney!"* and though it did not sound aloud this time, in the intensity of that call my lips must have moved.

Bassett made a slight motion with the revolver. "You'd better hurry up." As I moved dumbly to the chair, and once more gathered up the limp, sodden bundle, he showed his teeth in a fleeting grin.

"It won't do you any good to yell for help. If that fancy man of yours turns up, he won't have time to do anything. I'll see him coming. I'll pull this trigger before he can shoot me, and if I have to die you'll go first."

So that was it. No matter how it turned out, I was to be liquidated—because I knew his identity. How queer to think that if he had waited only a few minutes he would have heard me denouncing another person! But he didn't know that, and since he had now given himself away beyond any doubt, I had about five minutes to live.

It seems so wasteful, I thought, and automatically glanced around me.

The ugly, vulgar room was brightly lighted still. No doubt he had left it just as it was when he had made his ill-advised pilgrimage to my apartment; it would look the same if Bassett managed to escape detection and return to the closet. How on earth did he think he could do it? A shot anywhere would give the alarm.

But of course. The gun was only a threat. There would be one more blow on the head, silent and sure, and marked with the signature of the Cork; and the men who found my body would be forced to believe that the Cork was someone they had never seen—because Mr. Bassett, whom they had suspected, could not possibly have struck that blow.

Well, at that it might be better than a bullet, plowing and tearing through one's flesh, to be felt for an agonizing moment before one felt no more. Rigid with impotent anger, I stepped ahead of him into the dark rear entry.

For one moment a surge of incredulous hope lifted my heart, for I could have sworn that through the glass top of the rear door I had seen a shadowy figure that disappeared even as I glimpsed it. Then I felt the hard pressure of Bassett's gun against my shoulder blade.

No matter who came, no matter if Barney himself had miraculously turned up outside the apartment and heard what Bassett threatened, no matter if he should in answer to my silent cry be here at this moment, near to me, wanting to help—it would be of no use.

I caught my breath. After all, I had no particular desire to die.

"Turn to the left," said the soft whisper in my ear. I'd forgotten I was in stockinged feet, until the slimy cold of the alley paving struck them. Die with your boots on in everything but literal fact, I thought wearily, stepping painfully over the rough edges of cement blocks. The alley skirted the rear and north sides of the building, and mentally I picked out the place where the blow would fall: at the turn, some twenty feet ahead, where the angle of the passage bent toward the street. He would not let me get as far as the sidewalk. Out there a hint of dawn seeped through the blackness; but here, in the deep canyon between the buildings, night was still thick and solid.

"You can put down the kid here." The command was scarcely more than breathed. I stopped obediently, feeling for a nook that was comparatively sheltered. The rain pelted down mercilessly. When at last they found Melissa, would she be already too far gone, from drugs and exposure?

Why, I thought, this *can't* be happening. I'll wake up—

But I had thought that once already this evening.

Bassett, I knew, covered me with the gun even as I bent over. The sense of self-preservation was still working in my thoughts, icily clear. What if, after we'd gone a few yards more down the black cleft of the alley, I should pretend to faint? No, that would do me no good. Even if I knew that help was there, a helper could not be quick enough to take advantage of my momentary safety. How would the rescuer know when I planned to drop out of range?

"Go ahead," came the hot breath in my ear. We were eight feet from the corner; five feet—

If there's any chance, I thought, if I see the slightest loophole, I must try somehow to dodge, or run. A gamble's better than sure death, but I'll have to keep poised on this hair-trigger expectancy, not let down for a moment.

We took another step—two more, three more.

I believe I knew it when Bassett raised his arm to strike. There was an almost impalpable sweep of air across my back, and I remember thinking, "Here it comes."

From around the corner of the building a hand shot out and tapped me on the shoulder: the mental hair trigger clicked, and I fell flat on my face.

And hell broke loose above me as, instinctively, I flung myself aside, rolling and scrambling on the wet pavement. Bassett's gun spat viciously, once, and as the echoes crashed back from the walls that enclosed us, I heard the impact of the bullet on stone. In the next second something leaped like a panther at the man beside me.

The clawing, twisting mass on the ground thrashed toward me so that I could only shield my head and crowd my body into the angle of the wall. The crack of another shot seemed to pierce the eardrums.

And then there were feet, running, slipping in the dark, and the two beside me lay ominously still. Presently, part of the inert mass detached itself, slowly, and rose into the dimness. There was a sound of panting, heavy, slow breaths. The other shadowy forms were closing in.

"Got him," the standing figure said; and for the second time that night I almost fainted at the sound of Barney's voice. "Got him with a dirty tackle; his head—cracked on the pavement. Only hope—didn't kill him. Want him to get—what's coming to him."

Someone was helping me up, solicitously inquiring if I were hurt. The voice was strange. "Come along," it said soothingly, "we'll get you in."

"The baby," I croaked, and started at a tottering run toward the place where I had laid her down.

"Now, take it easy," the voice said. "We'll get her. There's no danger now."

No danger. It was over, then? That hideous moment I had just lived through, in the blackness and pouring rain, had marked the end?—But it must be all right, I thought dully. Barney wasn't shot after all. That sunken-eyed creature who, a minute since, was urging me to my death, is lying back there on the broken pavement. They've caught him. I don't have to die—

All of life was miraculously given back to me, and I couldn't take in the idea.

"It happened so *fast*," I said helplessly to the stranger whose hand supported my arm.

"Sure it did. That was the only way it could happen," said his soothing tone.

We must have stopped, I must have groped in the mud for the baby or shown him where it was, for he was carrying it as we went through the entry into the landlord's apartment. It seemed a matter of great wonder that the entry should smell exactly the same, and that the beaded lamp should burn undisturbed, casting a calm light on Mrs. Ulrichson's tidies. It was perhaps ten minutes since I had left this little cave of brightness; but who could measure the extent of the journey I had taken, believing I should not return?

"Now, that's right," the man said. "You sit down and rest." I sank into the cushions of the chesterfield, and sat gazing stupidly into space.

There had been no one in the room a minute since, and now there were men, talking, moving about. Were there three of them, or a dozen? Without moving I turned my eyes toward the door and saw Garwood; at least, it must have been he, for I thought the hooked nose was familiar. I had seen it silhouetted against a car window, hours ago, a lifetime ago. Some recollection stirred in me and I looked at his overcoat pockets. The folded paper was gone.

Time began to open and shut like a concertina. Now the room filled and emptied in a second, as if a film were being run too fast; now a great breathless pause seemed to hang between one word of a sentence and the next. Men spoke and were silent, and I tried dimly to understand what they had said and found they might as well have been speaking a foreign language.

There was a tall man in a shabby trench coat, who had not been here before. Heavy eyelids drooped over his dark eyes, and he looked at me under their lashes. I didn't remember anyone's taking the baby away from me, but someone must have done. He was holding her closely in his arms.

The word "Cleveland" came out of the buzzing of voices, and struck my ears and somehow found its way to my brain. That must be the baby's father, Melissa's father who had been looking for her—Mr. Cleveland was saying something to me. Of all things, he was kissing my hand.

"I don't believe she gets you, Chief," said Garwood's voice. I could hear that, as if muffling fog had lifted. "She's been through plenty. My Lord, when we found that ladder contraption and traced her through the next apartment and down the fire escape and in the window on the landing, I thought Barney'd go nuts. And then he was just about to walk in this door when he heard her talking, and knew—"

The fog came down again. Walter Cleveland had gone away and returned, and this time he didn't have the baby. I sat there, weaker than a yard of kittens, my head resting against the back of the sofa. There seemed no reason why I should ever get up, or move a hand, or think.

But that was it. I was trying not to think. Something was coming, something that would have to be dealt with, and I must ask a question whose answer I had no real desire to know.

It was coming now. In the knot of men by the door I saw one who towered half a head above the rest, the spread of whose shoulders I knew. Garwood was speaking to me, but I kept my eyes on that averted figure.

"All he could think of," Garwood said, "was that thousand-to-one chance, waiting for 'em at the corner. I don't know what made him believe it would work. I was afraid—but you sure caught on fast, Miss Ferris."

Then the broad shoulders swung toward me, and I met the light blue eyes. They seemed to hold no expression whatsoever.

It was a surprise to find that my voice still functioned. I said, "Barney. Thanks."

"Why," he said easily, moving nearer, "you needn't thank me. Anyone would have done the same. You're the one who deserves the gratitude."

"No," I said violently, turning my head aside.

"Oh, yes. You saved the baby, and through your mistake about Bassett, your stumbling into danger, we got him cold. We have proof now, even though we might not have chosen to get it in quite that way."

I said, "That's good."

He came up beside the sofa, and spoke in a low tone so that none of the men by the door could hear him. "It was you, I suppose, who let him out?"

With a last remnant of self-respect I forced my head around and my eyes up to his. "Yes," I said, "I let him out."

Then, as he said nothing, I brought out the question. Find out now, and have it over with.

"How did you know—to come? Did you know all the time he was—at large, or—"

It didn't seem to mean much, but he understood. Keeping his eyes on mine, he reached into his pocket and brought out a fold of newspaper.

"Garwood—found it?" I whispered.

Barney shook his head. "Nobody saw it but me," he said remotely, and spread out the folds.

Oh, yes, it was legible; it was all too legible. The sprawling letters of rose-red paste cut boldly across gray newsprint. "Barney is the Cork."

I tried to say, "I'm sorry," but before the words were shaped he was speaking again. There was nothing but curiosity in his eyes, but his voice was deadly cold, with that same paralyzing quality he had used on Colly O'Shea.

"You'd make a good poker player," he said. "You certainly put it over on me, from beginning to end."

I could only sit there limply, keeping my eyes on his by a violent effort of will.

"What I want to know is—" he said presently—and was interrupted by a hail from the door.

"Barney, here a minute? They want you to give—"

"Coming," Barney said, and turned on his heel and left.

There was another blank space after that. Between fatigue and pain and mortification, I was about down to rock bottom. Maybe I answered questions when they were asked me; I don't know. The thing I remember came at the very end of my sojourn in the landlady's apartment.

Mr. Cleveland, mysteriously reappeared, was sitting beside me, and Garwood stood by, writing something with an air of furious concentration. "I know it's too much to ask of you," Mr. Cleveland said. "The reporters are out there—"

I came to life with a jerk. "Please," I said wildly, "oh, please—not the papers. Couldn't you leave me out altogether? I was in it only by accident."

The editor gave me a singularly charming smile. "We can't leave you out," he said. "Not possible, I'm afraid."

"But I can't—I couldn't talk to anyone—oh, not now. Please."

Garwood cleared his throat, keeping his eyes on the paper in his hand. "Chief," he said in a low voice, "I know you promised the other papers a beat on this, for their help; but couldn't we save just a small part of it—?"

The heavy dark eyes turned to him, and then back to me. "It would be scarcely fair," Mr. Cleveland said in a voice torn by longing.

"Sure it's fair. Just this one angle for our first edition—we needn't mention her name till then. They've got the rest of the story."

"Miss Ferris does need a rest," the editor said. "And if she asks it as a favor—there's so little we can do to thank her—"

So that was why I didn't appear in the morning papers.

They helped me up after a few minutes, and I refused more help to get me to my apartment. No need now to race breathlessly up the three flights, nor to cower behind doors with a thumping heart. It was all over.

My door stood ajar. I went in, slow-footed with weariness, and surveyed the wreckage. The living room was in a stupendous clutter of ashes, newspapers, scattered sand and displaced furniture, and a chilly half-light crept around the edges of the drawn blind. It was drearier than campaign headquarters the morning after a lost election—and grotesque as the fancy of Salvador Dali, for someone had brought in the ladder and the ironing board and left them lolling drunkenly against the chesterfield.

I stared at the two wooden objects and saw them once more precariously balanced on wet windowsills. I measured with a horrified eye the space between the treads of the ladder, and remembered the sheer drop of four stories to the bottom of the light well; and I was shaken with a chill of mortal sickness.

All that's needed to complete this picture, I thought, is me in a dead faint in the middle of it.

The clock said half-past six. I turned my back on the desolation, packed a toothbrush and a change of clothing, and went downstairs to find a taxi that would take me to a hotel.

"Where'd I get those extra two dollars?" I thought, paying the cabman out of my sixty-seven cents: and then remembered that Barney had given me the money, nine hours ago, for this very purpose of going to a hotel. Maybe I could keep it for a souvenir; that, and a host of disturbing thoughts, would be about all I'd got out of my night's adventure.

I had to break into the two dollars, though, for breakfast. The meal wasn't worth it, seeming to be compounded of dust, ashes, and dead sea fruit under glass. No use sitting around bemoaning my lot. I went to the office, hearing as if from a long way off the shouts of newsboys along the road.

It was early, the office hadn't opened yet, but a number of my fellow-workers were gathered in the big outside room producing a deafening babble. "Right here in town—" "—even before the police so much as—" "—True after all, there *was* a Cork, and do you remember how everyone—" "—can't make out who this—"

Someone on the outskirts of the group waved a paper at me. "Did you see this, Miss Ferris?" The headlines read, in immense letters, "Kidnap, defense plot foiled."

It was cowardly, of course, but I felt in no condition to reveal my knowledge as yet. I'd put off the moment as long as possible. "Let's see," I cried, and snatched a section of the newspaper. It bore only the end of the story, afterthoughts of news to elaborate what had been described under the main heading. —The baby under a doctor's care, she was ill but would recover. —The police were to investigate the beating administered to the kidnappers; no one seemed to know who had done it. (You gathered that no one regretted it, and the police wouldn't look very long.) Tenants of "El Central" had been interviewed; Mrs. Ellaline Pitman, on the same floor as the kidnap hideout, had heard nothing during the night, but reported that her apartment had been mysteriously ransacked. The inexplicable part was that nothing was missing, though several valuable pieces of jewelry were in plain sight—

I looked up and met the hazel eyes of Roger Tripp, filled with excitement and awe. He brandished a paper of his own, and I followed his pointing finger to an address.

"Isn't that somewhere near your apartment house, Miss Ferris?"

I gave a little shriek, as if in astonishment. "Why, that *is* my apartment house," said I. "You don't mean that all this was—"

Roger nodded. "Of all places, that's where they had the baby hidden. I understand there was fighting, and of course the police were called in at the end and all the tenants were questioned. It must have been terrible. I—I can't help feeling glad you were in the country; that spared you a dreadful experience."

"So it did," I said, and gazed at him round-eyed. "How fortunate!"

The first excitement over, he gave me a friendly inspection. "I hoped to see you looking less tired. Wasn't the weekend a success?"

"Thank you, it was very restful—all except last night, when I didn't get much sleep."

"Oh, the storm?"

"Yes, that was it. The storm. I'll—I'll tell you all about it later."

Someone looked round a corner, and said, "S-s-st. The old man."

"Good heavens," Roger exclaimed, "it's after opening time!"

In thirty seconds the crowd had dispersed and the newspapers had been whisked into oblivion. All that Mr. Caya saw, as he stumped his way through the main room, was a department head quietly giving orders to the humblest of his file clerks.

"These are to be copied in triplicate, Miss Ferris," Roger was saying virtuously; then, as the old man's footsteps receded, he added, "We're busy this morning, I may not get another chance to ask if you'd care to take in a show with me tonight?"

For one moment I wavered; I might plead the need of rest, or say, "Wait till this afternoon and see how we both feel."

And then I knew it was no good, and never would be.

"Thank you, Mr. Tripp," I said, "but—I think not."

It was the end of *that*.

Mercifully, Caya and Co. were, as Roger had said, in for a busy morning. I filed and copied and cross-indexed like mad for three hours, but in doing so defeated my own purpose; for 11:30 came and there was no more work on my desk.

Mrs. Brent, whom I approached in Roger's absence, looked a bit startled at my demand for something to do. "Well," she said doubtfully, "there's this stack of letters to be put in the dead file. You know where that is?"

I knew: upstairs in a dusty inside room which the staff called the Black Hole of Calcutta. "Give 'em to me," I said.

She gave me a shrewd glance. "What's the matter, that you're so anxious for work? Had a spat with the boyfriend?"

"I haven't any boyfriends at all," I told her. "You might as well get that straight—all of you."

"Well," said Mrs. Brent, with a shrug, "of course, we *knew* you weren't acquainted with anyone in the city—except here in the office."

"That includes the office," said I, and stalked away with my hands full of antiquated correspondence.

That didn't last long enough either, though I dallied in the Black Hole as long as I could. The impulse to industry died also, and when I came out into the empty hall my steps lagged more and more slowly. I found myself standing there and gazing through a smudged window at the city of San Francisco, hating it, unutterably tired of myself, aching inside and out.

The wet, windy street, the gloomy canyons of gray buildings, looked just the same as they had the night before. I didn't mean a thing to them. Well, Cameron, you fooled yourself nicely, didn't you? You thought an adventure would set you up for life, solve your problems happily; you wished for it and you got it—and all the time what you wanted was to fall romantically in love and be loved in return. Without that, none of the rest matters.

This wasn't the sort of thing you got over. I knew, drearily, that this was the real thing, I could never accept anything else—and I'd thrown it away.

It had been so nearly within my grasp—literally only three inches away. I leaned my hot forehead against the window, and reflected on that.

—I wish I *had* fallen into his arms, I thought; I'd have that much at least—

A number of unsuitable things seemed all at once to be happening in the dingy corridor. The dead fatigue went from me like the dropping of a heavy weight. Several suns began to rise in a dazzle of red and gold, and a full orchestra and chorus burst into the *Ode to Joy*. All that I actually saw, of course, was Barney coming round the far end of the hall; all I had heard was his voice, saying my name.

He was no longer the unshaven, disreputable figure of the night before, he had changed to a well-made dark suit and topcoat. Also, he was angry.

—Oh dear, I thought, this is a very bad case. Whether he's furious or not, just to be near him seems enough—

"I couldn't find you," he said accusingly. "I never thought of your coming to the office; you just disappeared."

"How did you get up here?" I counter-attacked. "Nobody's supposed to be upstairs in this building, except the employees."

"I told them," he said coolly, "that I was a plainclothes man, and that I had to see you alone and before you could be warned."

"Oh, splendid," I said, wincing. "That will fix me up just right."

"I did have to see you. There's something I've got to say."

"Go ahead," I told him, bracing myself.

"Not out here," said Barney coldly, "in private. Where does that door lead to?"

Silently I opened the door of the Black Hole, and he followed me in. I found myself backed up against the filing cases on the far side of the room, as if I'd be safer at a distance. Hat in hand, he stood by the closed door.

"I owe you an apology," I said.

"No!" His disclaimer was almost savage. "Nothing of the kind, ever. I've been thinking it over, Cameron; I haven't thought of much else since I left you."

His hands were restless, those hands whose movements had always been quiet and sure. It was a shock to realize that he was not quite confident; but under scowling brows his eyes were direct.

"You made a mistake, but you retrieved it a thousand times over. And I know, of course, why you made it; because I'd lied to you at the very beginning. That colored everything that came after—didn't it?"

"Yes," I said, "but I should have known better just the same."

"Forget it," said Barney impatiently. "The way things turned out, I don't care if you thought I was Hitler. There's just one thing I had to know."

He paused and gave me a level look, no longer angry. "How long did you think it?" he asked urgently. "From the beginning, or—"

"No. The purple ink-pad fell out of your suitcase. I did think, then, that maybe you'd picked it up in the next apartment when you searched. That was right, wasn't it?"

He nodded slowly.

"And then I heard—I heard you and O'Shea, talking. I was up in the rafters, I didn't know it was you in the next room. And he—you said I knew nothing essential, but you'd see to it that I'd never talk—never say a word."

For a moment Barney looked puzzled, and then enlightenment spread gradually over his face, relaxing the bleak hardness of its lines.

"Colly," he said deliberately, "is not in debt to society—not at this moment; but for a short time last night, instinct was too strong for him."

The thing broke over me like a wave. "He was coming out of Mrs. Pitman's window, and you didn't want me to see him! And that's what you argued about—'Ice!' You made him put back those dia—"

He stopped me with a gesture. "Don't say it. You saw nothing. You don't know anything about him. Keep it like that. You see, he—he stacked up a little extra credit last night, but the law might not see it that way. He couldn't afford to get mixed up with any policemen.

"And what I told him was that if you were asked to keep the secret you'd do it. I knew you could be trusted."

"I had that coming," I said faintly, "but you're making me feel perfectly awful."

"Such was not the intention." He spoke gravely, but the blue eyes gave off a single spark of laughter. "I didn't want to—I meant to wait for a decent interval, maybe until I'd seen the aspidistra; but just now, when I heard what you said in the hall—"

"In the hall? *What* did I say?"

"Maybe I wasn't supposed to hear it. You said, 'I wish I had fallen into his arms.' Cameron, if I could possibly think you meant me—"

The words hung between us, echoing in the dusty air. My heart picked up their rhythm, beating it out slowly, strongly.

"I did," said I.

He looked at me in silence for a long minute. Then, "That changes all my plans," said Barney, and in two strides had covered the distance between us.

In the moment when his head bent to mine, I was shaken by one last pang of recurring doubt. After that I couldn't be bothered to think at all.

Coming back at last from interstellar space, getting my eyes open with a great effort, I saw that his face was drawn, frowning almost as if in pain. "You're so beautiful," the husky voice whispered.

The doubt left me, at once and forever. For the first time in my life I felt beautiful.

It seemed there was one thing yet to be settled. "Look, my dear," he said, "this is all over, you know; and there isn't much excitement or romance on a fruit ranch."

I said, "Not up to now, maybe."

We stepped out into the dingy corridor, and saw before us the gray panorama of the city. “Barney,” I said, “you see this place, this big indifferent town that looks as if it could defeat anyone?”

“Uh-huh.”

“I’ll take it the way Grant took Richmond.”

“That was a slow job,” he pointed out.

“I know. But he had confidence, didn’t he? Maybe you’re fishing, but I’ll tell you. It’s because I’m somebody’s mouse—”

“Have it your way, then. Because I’m your mouse—”

“Barney, not here! There’s somebody coming up the stairs—”

“Oh, well, I don’t care either—”

Long before the person on the stairs hove into sight, I knew who it was. Inevitably, the steps I had heard were made by the feet of Roger Tripp. Once more his kindly nature had led him to come to the rescue—this time not only unasked but unwanted.

He appeared at the far end of the hall, and paused. I suppose that to his nearsighted eyes we were just a blur, but when one blur slowly divides itself in two, even a myopic vision can gather that something goes on.

“Miss Ferris!” he called anxiously, “someone said—I wondered if you were all right, they said there was a policeman looking for you.”

All I could think of to say was, “He found me.” Dizzily I detached myself from Barney’s embrace, retaining a hold on his arm to steady me.

Roger waited uncertainly for a minute longer, and then began a dubious advance toward us.

(“Everyone knew you had no acquaintances here.”)

Poor Roger, I thought—so kind, so thoughtful of my reputation—the least I can do is to tell you the secret now—but I can’t shout it, I’ll wait till you come up—

I waited. The only thing on earth that seemed real was the arm that held me; everything else swam in a delirious haze; yet there was something I should say—something was lacking.

And then it came.

"Quick, Barney!" I demanded in a low voice that was almost strangled by sudden laughter. *"What's your name?"*